IN HER EYES

I saw the world slip away

First published in India on 06th October, 2024

Copyright © Naman Porwal 2024

ISBN 9798895880913

Diary Number 40978/2024-CO/L

ROC Number L-155974/2024

In Her Eyes

Based on true story

CONTENTS

Naman Porwal

In her eyes, I saw an illusion dancing with the rain

Naman Porwal

PREFACE

Beneath the veil of raindrops, where silence meets the storm, lies a story that isn't bound by time, but by the heart. **"In Her Eyes"** is a journey into the fragile spaces between love and illusion, where the lines between reality and dreams blur, leaving only the pulse of longing to guide the way. It's a story of love as fleeting as mist and as powerful as the downpour that shapes it.

Noah wasn't looking for answers when he met Stella, but in her eyes, he saw the world—an illusion so intoxicating it was impossible to turn away. She was his storm and his calm, a fragile soul wrapped in layers of desire and contradictions. Yet, with every moment they shared, there was something deeper, something unspoken—like the quiet rumble of thunder before the skies break open.

As rain swept through their lives, it wasn't just love they were battling, but the forces within themselves. Stella wanted to escape the past, to leave behind everything she once knew, while Noah stood rooted to the ground he called home. Could love survive such an impossible divide? Or was it always meant to be a fleeting illusion, a mirage that vanishes the moment you reach for it?

This is not just a love story—it is a dance with fate, a journey through heartbreak, hope, and the choices that linger long after the rain stops falling. What would you do if the person you loved became the one thing you could never truly have?

Prepare to lose yourself in the rain and in her eyes.

Naman Porwal

1. When she walked in

As Stella entered the classroom, the familiar sound of her voice and the intoxicating scent of her perfume washed over me like a tidal wave of memories. I couldn't help but be drawn to her, my eyes locking onto her figure as she made her way to the empty seat next to me.

But my fascination with Stella was nothing new. We had a history that stretched back to our high school days in Zermatt, my small hometown nestled in the heart of the Swiss Alps. Back then, Stella had been a force of nature, a whirlwind of intensity and passion that left an indelible mark on everyone she encountered.

Despite our differences, we had forged a friendship born out of mutual respect and admiration. Stella had sought me out, drawn to my quiet demeanour and unwavering loyalty. We had shared countless moments together, laughing, arguing, and dreaming of the future.

However, our paths diverged after high school. Stella's family had relocated to Grindelwald, another picturesque town nestled in the Swiss countryside, following her father's job opportunity. It was a bittersweet parting, marked by promises to stay in touch and hopes of reuniting one day.

And now, here she was, sitting beside me in a university classroom in Zurich, of all places. The irony of our reunion was not lost on me, and as I stole a glance at her, I couldn't help but wonder what twists of fate had brought us back together after all this time.

Her presence illuminated the room, and I couldn't help but be mesmerized by her radiance. With a warm smile, she greeted me, her eyes sparkling with surprise and delight.

"Hey, Noah! What a pleasant surprise to see you here," she exclaimed, her voice was like music to my ears.

Returning her smile, I extended my hand for a handshake, feeling a rush of nostalgia wash over me. "It's been a long time," I replied, my voice tinged with warmth.

Stella's laughter danced in the air as she nodded in agreement. "Indeed, it has. You know, Noah, you've grown quite handsome," she teased, her eyes twinkling mischievously.

Blushing slightly at her compliment, I chuckled and replied, "Well, thank you. And I must say, you've only become more beautiful with time."

"Aw, thanks," she said, her smile widening. "But enough about us. Let's focus on this lecture, shall we?"

As the lecture began and Stella's attention turned to the front of the classroom, I couldn't help but wander back to school days where we made so many memories. Five years ago, during our high school days in Zermatt, I was known as the introvert and reserved type, preferring the company of a few close friends. Despite my quiet demeanour, I cherished the friendships I had cultivated, especially the bond I shared with Stella.

Stella was a whirlwind of energy and excitement, always pushing the boundaries and dragging me along for the ride. We complemented each other in ways that made our friendship unique and enduring.

One of our favourite pastimes was bunking classes and exploring the town on my bike. With the wind in our hair and the freedom of the open road stretching out before us, we would set off on spontaneous adventures, discovering hidden gems and secret hideaways tucked away in the picturesque landscape of Zermatt.

Whether it was sneaking into abandoned buildings to uncover long-forgotten mysteries or simply lounging by the riverbank, lost in conversation and laughter, every moment spent with Stella was an adventure waiting to unfold.

There were moments of disappointment, of arguments and misunderstandings, but through it all, our friendship remained steadfast and unwavering.

From impromptu movie nights to shopping sprees at the local mall, Stella and I made the most of our high school days, creating memories that would last a lifetime.

After high school, Stella and I went our separate ways as she moved to Grindelwald with her family, while I remained in Zermatt. We stayed in touch sporadically, exchanging occasional messages and updates on our lives, but the distance between us made it difficult to maintain the same level of closeness we had shared during our school days.

In Her Eyes

As the years passed, Stella pursued her education in Grindelwald, eventually graduating and embarking on a new chapter of her life. Meanwhile, I focused on my studies in Zermatt, determined to carve out a path for myself in the world of finance.

Now, fate has brought us both to Zurich, the bustling city that serves as the backdrop for our latest adventure. We find ourselves enrolled in the same master's program in finance, each pursuing our professional aspirations in this vibrant metropolis.

I live in a private apartment with some college friends, relishing the independence and camaraderie that comes with shared living arrangements. Stella, on the other hand, resides in a private apartment with her friend Elena.

As we navigate the challenges and opportunities that come with pursuing our master's degrees, I can't help but wonder how our paths intertwined once again. Will our reunion in Zurich reignite the spark of friendship and camaraderie that defined our school days? Only time will tell.

The pulsating beat of the music reverberated through the air as Stella and I made our way to Mike's house for the freshman year party. The excitement was palpable as we approached the brightly lit house, the sounds of laughter and chatter growing louder with each step.

As we entered the crowded living room, my senses were overwhelmed by the sights and sounds of the lively gathering. People were packed shoulder to shoulder, their voices blending into a cacophony of laughter and conversation. Lights cast a warm glow over the room, creating an atmosphere of intimacy and camaraderie.

Stella's hand found mine in the sea of bodies, her touch sending a thrill of anticipation coursing through me. With a mischievous smile, she led me through the crowd, introducing me to her friends with infectious enthusiasm.

"Hey guys, this is Noah," she exclaimed, her voice barely audible over the din of the party. "Noah, meet Mike, Stephen, and Elena."

I exchanged polite greetings with Stella's friends, the warmth of their smiles putting me at ease amidst the pulsating energy of the party. With introductions out of the way, we dove headfirst into the festivities, the night unfolding in a whirlwind of laughter and revelry.

Drinking games were in full swing, the air thick with the heady scent of alcohol as cups clinked and laughter echoed off the walls. Stella and I found ourselves at the center of the action, our laughter mingling with the sounds of the party as we competed in game after game, the competitive spirit fueling our antics.

As the night wore on and the alcohol flowed freely, Stella and I found ourselves in a quiet corner of the house, away from the pulsating music and the raucous laughter of the party. The dim lighting cast a warm glow over us as we leaned in close, our words slurred and our inhibitions lowered by the intoxicating effects of the booze.

With a playful smirk, Stella nudged me teasingly, her eyes twinkling mischievously as she leaned in closer. "You know, Noah, I think you look pretty cute when you're tipsy," she said, her voice laced with amusement.

Chuckling softly, I met her gaze, feeling a rush of warmth spread across my cheeks at her compliment. "Well, you're not so bad yourself," I replied, my voice slightly unsteady but full of sincerity.

As the conversation flowed effortlessly between us, fueled by the heady combination of alcohol and attraction, our inhibitions melted away, leaving us open and vulnerable in each other's presence. With each shared laugh and lingering glance, the tension between us grew palpable, sparking a fire that threatened to consume us both.

Lost in the moment, I reached out to brush a stray lock of hair from Stella's face, my fingers lingering against her cheek as our eyes locked in a silent exchange of longing and desire. "Stella, you look beautiful," I said.

As the night stretched on and the party continued to rage on around us, Stella and I remained locked in our own little world, lost in the intoxicating dance of flirtation and attraction. Despite the raucous surroundings, our connection felt electric, the air charged with anticipation as we danced on the floor feeling carefree from the world.

As the days passed and Stella and I settled into our routine in Zurich, our interactions became more frequent, and our conversations more animated.

One day, after class, I caught up with Stella as she was packing up her belongings, a playful smile dancing on her lips.

"Hey, Noah! What are your plans for the evening?" she asked, her eyes sparkling with curiosity.

Shrugging nonchalantly, I replied, "Not much, just the usual. Probably heading back to the apartment to catch up on some reading."

Stella's expression brightened as she asked, "I heard there's a new café that just opened downtown. What do you say we check it out together?"

Caught off guard by her suggestion, I hesitated for a moment before nodding enthusiastically. "That sounds like a great idea! I'm in."

And so, we found ourselves wandering the misty, rain-kissed streets of Zurich, the air cool and damp as a light drizzle fell around us. Fog curled around the buildings, softening the colorful facades as we laughed and talked, exploring the quiet corners of the city. The gentle patter of rain on cobblestone accompanied us as we stumbled upon a quaint café hidden in a charming alley. Inside, over steaming cups of coffee and slices of cake, we shared stories and dreams, the warmth between us growing as the hours slipped away unnoticed, lost in each other's company.

As nightfall settled in, the dark clouds thickened, and the streetlights flickered on, casting a dim glow over the rain-soaked streets. The moon barely peeked through the overcast sky, and the cold breeze carried the scent of rain. Stella turned to me under the shadow of the streetlight, her face illuminated by its soft amber glow. A gentle smile curled on her lips, her eyes reflecting the faint lights of the city.

"Noah," she said softly, her voice breaking through the stillness of the night. "I had such a wonderful time today. We should do this more often." Her words, warm against the chill in the air, made the moment feel timeless.

I couldn't agree more. "Absolutely," I replied, returning her smile.

And so, from that day forward, Stella and I made a habit of spending time together, whether it was exploring new cafes, strolling through the park, or simply enjoying each other's company. Our daily hangouts became the highlight of my day, a source of joy and camaraderie that I treasured more than words could express.

As my friendship with Stella and her friends deepened, our lives became increasingly intertwined, filled with shared laughter, inside jokes, and unforgettable moments. Elena quickly became one of my closest confidants, her easygoing nature and quick wit making her a joy to be around. It wasn't long before she and Mike found themselves drawn to each other, their budding romance adding an extra layer of warmth and camaraderie to our tight-knit group.

Stella and I grew closer with each passing day, as we shared the minutiae of our lives and the dreams that fueled our passions. Whether it was over a cup of coffee in our favorite café or a leisurely stroll through the picturesque streets of Zurich, we found solace in each other's company, our conversations flowing effortlessly as we explored the depths of our hearts and minds.

As the crisp October air kissed our cheeks, I couldn't help but feel a sense of exhilaration coursing through my veins as Stella and I embarked on our impromptu adventure to Uetliberg mountain.

"Where are we going?" Stella asked, her curiosity piqued as she straddled the back of my bike, her arms wrapped securely around my waist.

"It's a surprise," I replied with a grin, the wind whipping through my hair as we navigated the winding roads leading up to the mountain.

The chill air nipped at our skin as we made our way up the mountain, the vibrant hues of autumn painting the landscape in shades of gold and crimson. With each twist and turn of the road, the anticipation build within us.

As we finally reached the base of the mountain and began our ascent on foot, the sheer beauty of the landscape wrapped around us like a dream. The towering peaks of the Swiss Alps loomed majestically in the distance, their snow-capped summits glowing faintly under the muted sunlight, breaking through the thick clouds. The trees around us whispered softly in the wet, foggy air, their leaves glistening from the drizzle. The cold breeze nipped at our skin, sending a chill down my spine as it tousled our hair, carrying the fresh scent of pine and rain.

I couldn't help but steal glances at Stella. She moved with ease, her face glowing in the soft, damp light, her eyes sparkling with excitement despite the cold. The misty rain kissed her cheeks, adding a natural flush to her skin. I marveled at how effortlessly beautiful she looked amidst the wild, untamed beauty of the mountains, her energy matching the landscape's quiet intensity. Each stolen glance made me fall just a little deeper into the moment, wishing it would stretch on forever.

Stella's laughter echoed in the crisp mountain air as she bounded ahead of me, her enthusiasm infectious as she urged me to keep up. She stopped for me as I couldn't keep up and sat at the stone.

"Let's go Noah," she said from few steps ahead.

"Let's take a break," I said.

She came to me and offered me her hand.

In Her Eyes

"Take my hand and don't let it go," she said.

I took her hand and we went further up. With her hand in mine, I felt a surge of warmth spread through me, a sense of connection and intimacy that transcended words. With each step we took, I found myself falling more and more under Stella's spell, the beauty of the landscape mirrored in the depths of her eyes.

And as we finally reached the summit, the breathtaking vista spread out before us like a painting come to life, I couldn't help but feel a sense of awe wash over me. But it was the sight of Stella, her eyes alight with wonder and joy, that truly took my breath away.

In that moment, as the sun dipped below the horizon and the world around us faded into shadow, I knew with a certainty that I would carry this memory with me for the rest of my days. For in the beauty of that mountaintop, in the warmth of Stella's touch, I had found something truly precious and irreplaceable.

Stella's phone rang repeatedly, and each time, the name "Paul" flashed across the screen. When she finally answered, I couldn't help but feel like she was being pulled further away from me, as if Paul had taken a part of her that I couldn't reach. I sat there quietly as she answered the call, her voice soft and calm as she talked to him. The conversation seemed to go on forever, and with each passing minute, a small knot of frustration began to form inside me. I tried to brush it off, but the lingering fear of losing her tugged at the back of my mind, making it hard to ignore.

As we descended the mountain in the fading light of the evening, the tension that had simmered beneath the surface threatened to boil over, casting a shadow over the beauty of our surroundings. But as the sun dipped below the horizon and the world around us was cloaked in darkness, I knew that I couldn't let my jealousy consume me. Taking a deep breath, I turned to Stella, determined to put my feelings into words.

"Stella, what is your passion in life?" I asked, my voice tinged with curiosity and a hint of apprehension.

"I want to go abroad and settle in USA," she said.

Stella's response was met with a sense of unease that settled in the pit of my stomach. Her desire to leave everything behind and start anew in the USA sent a shiver down my spine.

"But your family and friends are here," I protested, my words laced with a sense of longing and desperation.

"I just want to experience life, Noah," she explained, her voice gentle but resolute. "I've spent my whole life here, and now I want to see what else the world has to offer."

Her words struck a chord deep within me, stirring feelings of fear and uncertainty that I struggled to suppress. The thought of Stella leaving filled me with a sense of dread, a gnawing sense of emptiness threatening to consume me at the mere prospect of being left behind.

We reached her apartment and bid each other goodbye.

"It felt good going with you to the mountains today, Noah," she had said, her voice tinged with genuine warmth and affection.

"It's my pleasure," I said.

As I rode back to my apartment, I couldn't help but feel a sense of sadness wash over me at the thought of parting

In Her Eyes

ways. But amidst the bittersweet farewells and lingering glances, there was a spark of hope, a glimmer of possibility that perhaps, just perhaps, our paths would cross again in the future.

We started spending time together daily. The pang of jealousy that gnawed at my heart whenever Stella's phone lit up with the name "Paul" became an all too familiar sensation, a constant reminder of the invisible presence that loomed over our friendship.

Time and time again, I found myself eager for Stella's attention, only to be sidelined by the allure of her phone screen and the voice of a man. Each time she answered his call, I felt a pang of longing and frustration gnawing at my insides, a bitter taste of jealousy tainting the sweetness of our moments together.

I tried to push aside my feelings of insecurity and doubt, telling myself that I had no right to question Stella's friendships or her past. But as the calls became more frequent and their conversations stretched into the wee hours of the night, I found myself unable to ignore the gnawing sense of unease that lingered in the pit of my stomach.

Finally, unable to contain my curiosity any longer, I mustered the courage to broach the subject with Stella, my voice tinged with apprehension as I dared to ask the question that had been weighing on my mind for so long.

"Who is Paul?" I asked, my words hesitant and unsure.

Stella's eyes flickered with surprise at my question, her expression momentarily guarded before softening into a smile as she spoke. "Oh, Paul? He's just a good friend from school. He is well settled in New York and running his own company," she replied, her tone casual and nonchalant.

Her words did little to assuage the knot of insecurity that had formed in the pit of my stomach, but I forced myself to nod in understanding, swallowing down the bitter taste of jealousy that threatened to overwhelm me. In that moment, I realized that Stella's connection with Paul ran deeper than I had initially suspected, a realization that left me feeling more than a little unsettled. But I pushed aside my doubts and fears, choosing instead to focus on the present moment and the fragile bond that tethered us together, uncertain of what the future held for us or the role that Paul would play in our unfolding story.

As the weeks passed and Stella's conversations with Paul grew longer and more frequent, I found myself increasingly torn between the conflicting emotions that waged war within me. The gnawing sense of jealousy and insecurity that had plagued me since the first time I heard his name echoed in the depths of my heart, threatening to consume me with each passing day.

Unable to contain my turmoil any longer, I sought solace in the company of Elena, my closest confidant and dearest friend. We became close friends in the wake of Stella's never-ending calls with Paul, finding comfort and understanding in each other's presence.

One evening, as we, Mike, Elena, Stella and I sat together in the dimly lit confines of Elena's apartment, the weight of my emotions pressed heavily upon me as Stella was on her call with Paul. Elena turned to me with a knowing look in her eyes.

"You love her, don't you?" she asked softly, her voice gentle but probing.

In Her Eyes

Caught off guard by her question, I could only stare at her with wide eyes, the truth of her words hanging heavy in the air between us. With a heavy sigh, I nodded slowly, the weight of my confession lifting a burden from my chest even as it filled me with a sense of vulnerability.

Elena's expression softened with understanding as she reached out to place a comforting hand on my shoulder. "It's okay, Noah. You don't have to hide your feelings from me," she said reassuringly. "I've noticed the way you look at Stella, the way you light up whenever she's around. It's clear to me that your feelings run deeper than friendship."

Her words struck a chord deep within me, stirring feelings of longing and uncertainty that I had long tried to suppress. And as I poured out my heart to Elena, sharing every little detail of my feelings for Stella and the turmoil that had consumed me in recent weeks, I found solace in her unwavering support and understanding.

But it was Elena's next words that sent a shiver down my spine, a cold realization dawning on me like a bolt from the blue. "I think there's something more than just friendship between Stella and Paul," she confided, her voice tinged with concern. "And I fear that you may be caught in the crossfire of a love triangle that's already begun to unravel."

2. When truth meets silence

The cool night air enveloped us as Stella and I sat alone on the rooftop of her apartment, the distant city lights twinkling in the darkness below. The weight of my emotions hung heavy in the air between us, a silent testament to the turmoil that had been brewing within me for weeks. Unable to contain my growing unease any longer, I took a deep breath and mustered the courage to broach the subject that had been weighing on my mind.

"Stella, I need to ask you something," I began, my voice tinged with desperation and insecurity. "Is there something between you and Paul? You talk to him so much on the phone."

Stella's eyes widened in surprise at my question, her expression momentarily guarded before softening into a look of understanding. "No, Noah, there's nothing between me and Paul," she replied, her voice gentle but firm. "We're just good friends, that's all. He doesn't have anybody else to talk to, so I try to be there for him."

Her words did little to ease the knot of anxiety that had formed in the pit of my stomach, but I forced myself to nod in understanding, swallowing down the bitter taste of jealousy that threatened to overwhelm me. I was not convinced but that's all I got there. Maybe, Paul likes her and that's why he calls her so much.

"I just want you to be present with us, to spend time with your friends and enjoy the moment," I explained, trying to make her see how much it mattered.

But before I could dwell on my insecurities any longer, Stella's tone turned defensive, her words laced with a hint of frustration and jealousy. "Why does it matter so much to you, Noah?" she retorted, her voice tinged with exasperation. "You're good friends with Elena, aren't you? Why do you need me?"

Her words cut me like a knife, leaving me speechless and reeling from the sting of her taunt. I struggled to find the right words to convey the depth of my feelings about her.

"Because Stella, we have a different bond, one that's special and unique. You do matter to me, you know," I said with wet eyes that she couldn't see in the dark.

Stella's demeanour softened after hearing my words, her eyes filled with genuine concern.

"I'm sorry, Noah. I didn't mean to upset you," she said softly, her voice filled with regret. "I'll try to talk less to Paul and spend more time with you and the others. I promise."

Her words were like a lifeline, pulling me back from the brink of despair and filling me with a sense of hope and reassurance. And as we sat together on that rooftop, bathed in the soft glow of the moonlight, I felt a newfound sense of security wash over me, knowing that Stella was by my side and that our bond was stronger than any fleeting doubts or insecurities.

With my head resting gently on Stella's shoulder, I stole a glance at her, marvelling at the way the moonlight danced in her eyes, casting a soft glow over her features. The warmth of Stella's shoulder beneath my head was a comforting anchor as we gazed out at the twinkling lights of the city below, the soft hum of the night enveloping us in a cocoon of tranquility. In that moment, all my doubts and fears melted away, replaced by a sense of contentment and peace that I had longed for.

"You know, Noah, I never realized how beautiful the city looks from up here," Stella mused, her voice soft and contemplative. "It's like a whole other world, just waiting to be explored."

I couldn't help but smile at her words, feeling a sense of warmth and contentment wash over me at the realization that Stella was finally beginning to open up to me, her walls crumbling in the face of our shared vulnerability.

As our friendship blossomed into something deeper, I found myself irresistibly drawn to Stella's presence, craving her companionship like a parched wanderer in the desert yearns for water. We spent countless hours together, both alone and in the company of our friends, creating memories that would last a lifetime.

As soon as we reached the restaurant, the rain began to fall, tapping gently against the windows. Inside, the warm glow of candlelight filled the room, reflecting off the droplets streaking down the glass. Stella and I sat across from each other at the table, and as the soft light danced on her face, I couldn't help but be struck by her beauty. In her black attire, she looked stunning, her elegance radiating effortlessly. My heart skipped a beat as I took in the moment, completely captivated by her presence.

Lost in her presence, I found myself forgetting the world around us as we shared laughter and conversation, our words dancing in the air like the flickering flames of the candles that adorned our table.

In those stolen moments of solitude, when it was just the two of us, I found myself falling deeper and deeper under Stella's spell. Her simplicity captivated me, her every word and gesture imbued with a quiet elegance and grace that left me breathless.

I marveled at the way she talked, her words weaving a tapestry of stories and dreams that drew me in like a moth to a flame. Her laughter was like music to my ears, filling the air with its infectious melody and warming my heart with its sweet sincerity.

And oh, how I adored the way she dressed, her fashion sense a reflection of her unique personality and inner beauty. Whether she was dressed to the nines for a night out on the town or lounging in casual attire at home, Stella exuded an effortless charm and confidence that left me spellbound.

But more than anything else, it was Stella herself who captured my heart completely and irrevocably. I loved the way she was, unapologetically herself in every moment, her authenticity shining through in everything she did.

In her presence, I felt alive in a way I had never felt before, my heart overflowing with a love so pure and all-encompassing that it took my breath away. I knew then, with a certainty that defied explanation, that I was head over

Naman Porwal

heels in love with Stella, and that I would do anything to be with her, now and forever.

As the evening came to a close and we stood together outside her apartment, the rain had settled into a gentle drizzle, adding a layer of intimacy to the moment. The soft glow of the streetlights cast a golden hue over us, and the air felt charged with unspoken words and lingering emotions. The city sounds seemed distant, muffled by the heaviness of anticipation that hung between us.

I took a deep breath, feeling the weight of the moment press down on me. My mind raced with the countless times I had wanted to say these words, and now, with my heart pounding in my chest, I knew I couldn't keep my feelings bottled up any longer. My voice was unsteady, betraying the nerves that twisted within me.

"Stella," I began, the rain creating a rhythmic backdrop as it tapped softly on the pavement, "I... I love you." My words were barely more than a whisper, but they carried the weight of every emotion I had been holding inside. "I've loved you from the moment you walked into that classroom, from the very first time I saw you. And... I want to be with you, for you, always."

I searched her eyes, hoping to find a glimmer of understanding, a sign that she might feel the same. My hands trembled slightly as I spoke, and I felt vulnerable, exposed under the gentle rain that seemed to echo the depth of my feelings. The world around us faded, leaving just the two of us standing there, caught in a moment that felt both exhilarating and terrifying.

As I poured my heart out to Stella, confessing my deepest feelings and laying bare my soul before her, the air between us crackled with tension and anticipation. But as the seconds stretched into minutes, I couldn't help but feel a sense of unease creeping into the depths of my being.

As the evening darkened around us, the rain continued to fall in a gentle, persistent drizzle, adding a sheen to the pavement and creating a soft mist that wove around us. The world seemed to narrow to just the two of us, wrapped in the cocoon of rain and dim streetlights.

Stella's expression remained inscrutable as she stood there, her gaze fixed on the wet pavement. The silence stretched out, thick and heavy, filled with the sound of rain pattering against the concrete and the occasional distant hum of city life. It was as if the rain was absorbing every word, leaving only the weight of my confession suspended in the damp air.

I felt every second of that silence as though it was stretching into eternity. My heart pounded loudly in my chest, each beat resonating with the tension of waiting for her response. I swallowed hard, the lump in my throat growing larger, threatening to choke me as I braced myself for what was to come.

Finally, Stella looked up, her eyes reflecting the muted glow of the streetlights and the raindrops glistening on her lashes. "Noah, how did this happen?" Her voice was soft, trembling slightly as it broke the silence. "I... I appreciate your honesty," she continued, her tone filled with a mixture of regret and uncertainty. "But I... I need some time to think about this."

Her words hit me like a sudden gust of wind, chilling and unexpected. They were not the affirmations I had hoped for, but rather a plea for time and space to process what I had just laid bare. The mist swirled around us, as if it too was trying to wrap its arms around the moment, softening the harshness of her response.

I stood there, feeling the rain mix with my tears, the cold seeping into my bones as I tried to make sense of the situation. The world outside seemed to blur into a watercolour of wet and grey, mirroring the tumultuous storm that had just erupted within me.

But even as my heart sank, a glimmer of hope flickered deep within me, a small voice whispering that perhaps, just perhaps, Stella needed time to come to terms with her own feelings. And so, with a heavy heart and a sense of resignation, I nodded slowly, accepting her words with a silent nod.

"Of course, Stella," I replied, my voice barely above a whisper. "Take all the time you need."

And with that, we parted ways, the weight of uncertainty hanging heavy in the air as I made my way back to my apartment, the echoes of my confession lingering in the darkness like a ghost.

As I walked onto the college campus the next day, my heart heavy with uncertainty, I could not shake the feeling of impending dread that seemed to hang over me like a dark cloud. And when Stella approached me, her expression somber and resigned, I knew that the decisive moment had finally arrived.

"Noah, I need to talk to you," she began, her voice barely above a whisper as she met my gaze with eyes filled with regret. "I... I can't be with you. I am already in a relationship... with Paul."

In Her Eyes

The words hit me like a sledgehammer, the shock and disbelief washing over me in waves as I struggled to comprehend what she was saying. My mind raced, my heart aching with a pain so profound that it threatened to consume me whole.

"But... but why, Stella?" I managed to choke out, my voice thick with emotion as I fought to hold back the tears threatening to spill from my eyes. "Why didn't you tell me sooner?"

Stella's gaze faltered, her eyes betraying a hint of guilt as she searched for the right words to say. "I... I didn't know how to tell you," she admitted, her voice barely audible over the din of the bustling campus. "I didn't want to hurt you, Noah. But I can't deny my feelings for Paul. I'm sorry."

Her words were like a knife to the heart, each syllable cutting deeper than the last as I struggled to come to the reality of the situation. And as Stella turned to walk away, leaving me standing there alone with my shattered dreams and broken heart, I felt a sense of devastation wash over me like a tidal wave.

With a heavy heart and a soul weighed down by grief, I turned and made my way out of the campus, the world around me blurring into a haze of pain and despair.

I mounted my bike and rode away, seeking refuge in the serene embrace of the mountains. The mist clung to the air, wrapping around me in a cool, comforting shroud as I ascended the winding roads. The rhythmic hum of the bike's wheels against the damp pavement was the only sound that accompanied me, blending with the whispering rustle of the trees and the gentle patter of rain.

Naman Porwal

I reached a quiet, secluded spot among the rocks, where the mist was thick and ethereal, like a soft, silvery curtain that blurred the world beyond. I dismounted and settled onto a cold, weathered stone, the chill seeping through my clothes as I stared out into the fog-shrouded expanse.

Time seemed to lose its meaning as I sat there, enveloped by the mist and darkness, my thoughts swirling in a tempest of confusion and heartache. The peaceful solitude of the mountains offered no answers, only a silent witness to my turmoil.

It wasn't until my phone rang that I was jolted back to reality. The screen displayed Elena's name, a reminder of the support I had, yet the thought of her voice felt like an intrusion into my solitude. I ignored the call, too weary to engage, needing to be alone in my thoughts and the embrace of the mist.

Eventually, I stood up, the darkness of night now fully settled around me, and began the descent back to my apartment. The rain had eased, leaving behind a glistening, reflective surface on the streets. When I arrived home, I sought out a cozy corner in my room, the comforting dimness and warmth a stark contrast to the cold, damp world outside. There, wrapped in a cocoon of solitude, I let my thoughts drift back to Stella, grappling with the echoes of our conversation and the ache of her absence.

3. Shattered pieces

As I sat alone in my apartment, lost in the depths of my grief, the sound of a knock at the door shattered the heavy silence that enveloped me like a suffocating blanket. With a heavy heart, I rose from my seat and made my way to answer it, the weight of the world pressing down on my shoulders like a burden too heavy to bear.

Opening the door, I was met with the solemn faces of Elena and Mike, their expressions mirroring the pain and sorrow that weighed heavily upon my own soul. Without a word, they stepped inside, their presence a silent testament to the depth of their concern and compassion.

"It's okay, Noah," Elena whispered, her voice soft and soothing as she enveloped me in a warm embrace. "We're here for you."

Tears stung my eyes as I buried my face in Elena's shoulder, the floodgates of my emotions finally breaking free as I allowed myself to grieve for the love that was lost. And as Elena held me close, offering comfort in the midst of my despair, I felt a sense of gratitude wash over me for the friends who stood by my side in my darkest hour.

But amidst the warmth of their embrace, there lingered a sense of guilt and regret that gnawed at the edges of my consciousness like a festering wound. "I love her," I choked out, my voice raw with emotion as I confessed the depth of my feelings to my friends.

Elena's arms tightened around me, her touch a balm to my wounded soul. "I warned you, Noah," she murmured softly, her words tinged with regret. "But still, you didn't stop."

I felt the weight of her words like a physical blow, the harsh reality of my own foolishness crashing down upon me with a force that left me reeling. "I had already fallen for her," I whispered, my voice barely above a whisper. "By the time I realized, it was too late."

Mike stepped forward, his expression grave as he placed a reassuring hand on my shoulder. "You need to forget her, Noah," he said, his voice firm and resolute. "She do this to everyone."

I wanted to protest, to defend Stella and the love that still burned brightly within my heart. But as I looked into the eyes of my friends, their concern and compassion shining through the darkness, I knew that they were right.

And so, with a heavy heart and a soul weighed down by sorrow, I nodded in silent agreement, knowing that the road ahead would be long and fraught with pain. But with Elena and Mike by my side, I knew even in my darkest hour, I was not alone.

As days turned into weeks, I found solace in the company of Elena and Mike, their unwavering support helping to ease the ache in my heart and fill the void left by Stella's absence. Together, we forged new friendships and created memories that helped to dull the pain of lost love.

One evening, as we gathered at a local café, laughter and conversation flowing freely between us, Stella made a rare appearance, her presence sending a ripple of tension through the air. Although, I saw her from far at campus but it has been months since we all sat together. But despite the lingering awkwardness, we welcomed her with open arms, eager to bridge the gap that had formed between us.

"Hey, Noah, Elena, Mike, it's good to see you all," she greeted us with a tentative smile.

My heart pounding in my chest as I braced myself for response. "Hi Stella," I said.

For a while, we managed to maintain a semblance of normalcy, catching up on each other's lives and reminiscing about old times. But as the conversation flowed, I couldn't shake the feeling of unease that settled over me like a dark cloud, the knowledge of Stella's lingering feelings for Paul casting a shadow over our interactions.

And as I exchanged a knowing glance with Elena and Mike, the weight of reality settling over me like a heavy blanket, I knew that despite my best efforts, some wounds were destined to remain unhealed, a painful reminder of the love that was lost.

As Elena and Mike excused themselves and stepped to the balcony facing river, leaving Stella and me alone, a palpable tension hung in the air, thick with unspoken words and unresolved emotions. For a moment, neither of us spoke, the weight of our shared history casting a shadow over the space between us.

But then, tentatively, Stella broke the silence, her voice soft and hesitant as she reached out to bridge the gap that had formed between us. "So, Noah, how have you been?" she asked, her eyes searching mine for any sign of warmth or familiarity.

I swallowed hard, the lump in my throat threatening to choke me as I struggled to find the right words to say. "I've been... okay," I replied, my voice barely above a whisper as I avoided meeting her gaze. "Just... trying to keep busy, you know?"

Stella nodded, her expression tinged with understanding as she reached out to touch my arm in a gesture of comfort. "I understand," she murmured softly. "It hasn't been easy for any of us."

For a moment, the weight of her words hung heavy in the air between us. And as we sat in silence, lost in our own thoughts, I couldn't help but feel a sense of longing stirring within me, a yearning for the connection that we had once shared.

But then, just as quickly as it had come, the moment passed, and Stella shifted uncomfortably in her seat, her eyes darting away from mine as she struggled to find the right words to say. "Noah, I... I know things have been awkward between us lately," she began, her voice tinged with regret. "But I want you to know that I'm here for you, okay? Whatever you need, I'm here."

I forced a small smile, my heart aching with the knowledge that despite her best intentions, Stella could never truly understand the depth of my pain. "Thanks,

In Her Eyes

Stella," I replied, my voice hollow with resignation. "I appreciate it."

"Noah, I need to tell you something," she began, her voice tinged with a hint of nervousness as she met my gaze with uncertainty. "I... I broke up with Paul."

Her words hit me like a bolt from the blue, the weight of her confession sinking in as I struggled to process the implications of what she had just said. But even as a sense of relief washed over me, I couldn't help but feel a twinge of uncertainty gnawing at the edges of my consciousness.

"Oh... I see," I replied, my voice carefully neutral as I fought to keep my emotions in check. "Are you okay?"

Stella nodded, her expression somber as she toyed with the rim of her coffee cup. "Yeah, I think so," she murmured softly. "It's been a long time coming, you know? But I think it's for the best."

I reached out to touch her hand in a gesture of comfort, my heart aching at the sight of her pain. "I'm sorry, Stella," I said softly, my voice laced with sympathy. "Breakups are never easy."

She offered me a small smile, her eyes shining with gratitude as she squeezed my hand in return. "Thanks, Noah," she replied, her voice thick with emotion. "I appreciate your support."

And as we sat together in companionable silence, the weight of her confession hanging heavy in the air between us, I couldn't help but feel a sense of hope stirring within me. Perhaps, just perhaps, this newfound freedom would pave the way for a fresh start for both of us, a chance to rebuild our friendship on a stronger foundation than ever before.

As days turned into weeks, Stella and I fell back into our old routine, the ease of our friendship slowly erasing the distance that had formed between us. We spent countless hours together, talking and laughing as if no time had passed at all.

Each day, I made it a routine to drop her home, taking her to shopping and refusing to let her spend a single cent. And as we studied together, her expertise in certain subjects proved invaluable, her guidance helping me navigate the complexities of our coursework with ease.

As the clock struck midnight, casting the world outside into darkness, I found myself immersed in conversation with Stella, the soft glow of my phone illuminating the dimly lit room as we spoke on call. The topic of our discussion had turned to the mundane details of daily life, the absence of our usual cook and the resulting dilemma of what to do for dinner.

Little did I know that Stella was listening intently to our conversation, her heart stirred by the realization that I have not had dinner. And so, without hesitation, she made her way to my apartment, I heard a knock on my door at 1 in the morning. As I opened the door, I found Stella standing outside in the late hours of the night. "Hey, Stella, what happened?" I asked, my voice filled with genuine curiosity.

With a smile that lit up the room, she stepped inside, her eyes sparkling with determination. "I wanted to spend some time with you," she replied simply, her words carrying a warmth that enveloped me like a comforting embrace.

I couldn't help but be taken aback by her sudden appearance, by the fact that she had come all the way to be with me. "At this time of the day?" I questioned, my eyebrows furrowing in confusion.

But Stella simply brushed aside my concerns with a dismissive wave of her hand. "Have you eaten something?" she inquired, her voice soft yet firm. When I admitted that I hadn't, she wasted no time in taking charge of the kitchen, her determination unwavering as she declared, "okay, wait, let me cook some food for you and your friends."

"But they fell asleep, it's just you and me," I said.

And so, with a newfound sense of appreciation for her kindness and generosity, I watched in awe as Stella set to work in the kitchen, her movements graceful and sure as she prepared a meal with all the love and care of a seasoned chef. And as the tantalizing aroma of her cooking filled the air, I knew that this unexpected gesture of friendship would be a memory I would cherish for years to come.

After dinner, as we sat together on couch, enjoying the warmth of each other's presence, Stella suddenly rose from her seat, her eyes alight with excitement and adventure. "Let's go on a long drive to the Swiss Alps," she exclaimed, her voice filled with enthusiasm.

I couldn't help but be taken aback by her spontaneous suggestion. "At this time?" I questioned, my eyebrows furrowing in uncertainty.

But Stella's determination was unwavering as she nodded eagerly. "Yes, let's go," she replied with a smile. "And don't worry about your driving skills, I'll teach you along the way."

Naman Porwal

With her reassurance echoing in my ears, I found myself unable to resist her infectious enthusiasm. And so, without further hesitation, we set off into the night, the hum of the engine and the soft glow of the dashboard filling the car with a sense of anticipation and excitement.

4. Moments of bliss

As Stella patiently guided me through the intricacies of driving, her calm presence by my side filled me with a sense of comfort and reassurance. And as we navigated the winding roads that led us towards the majestic Swiss Alps, I couldn't help but feel a sense of awe at the beauty of the world around us.

The moon cast its gentle light upon the snow-capped peaks, bathing them in an ethereal glow that seemed to illuminate the darkness of the night. And as the melody of Calum Scott's 'You Are the Reason' filled the car, I felt a surge of emotion welling up within me, a poignant reminder of the connection that bound us together.

As the car came to a stop on the winding mountain road, we stepped out into the cool night air, our breath forming misty clouds in the darkness. The soft glow of the car's headlights illuminated the rugged landscape, casting long shadows that danced across the rocky terrain.

We stood there, side by side, our eyes fixed on the majestic beauty of the Swiss Alps stretched out before us. The towering peaks loomed overhead, their snow-capped summits glistening in the moonlight like beacons guiding us towards our dreams.

In that moment, surrounded by the vastness of nature and the silence of the night, I felt a sense of wonder and awe wash over me. It was as if time itself had stood still, allowing us to bask in the sheer magnificence of the world around us.

In that fleeting moment, I felt as though I were living in a dream, a surreal and magical world where anything was possible. And as I looked into Stella's eyes, I knew that this was where I belonged, by her side, under the vast expanse of the night sky, with nothing but our love to guide us forward.

For in that moment, I realized that I couldn't bear to lose her, not now, not ever. She was my anchor in a world of uncertainty, my guiding light in the darkness. And as we danced beneath the stars, I made a silent vow to cherish every moment with her, to hold her close and never let her go.

In the soft glow of the moonlight, we sat side by side near the mountain, gazing up at the sky, which was dotted with countless stars. The breathtaking view of the galaxy stretched out before us, while the moonlight gently kissed the snow-capped peaks, its reflection shimmering across the mountains like a silver veil.

She rested her head on my shoulder, her warmth blending with the cool night air. The mist that lingered around us created a dreamlike atmosphere, as if we were the only two souls in the universe at that moment. The closeness between us intensified, the space that once

In Her Eyes

separated us vanished, replaced by the unspoken connection and the electric pulse of desire coursing through the air.

Each heartbeat echoed in the silence, the night sky witnessing the quiet, profound bond growing between us. We sat there, enveloped by the beauty of the moment, feeling like we were part of something timeless and eternal.

There were no vehicles on the road, and the night was peaceful, the only sounds being the rustling leaves and the faint whisper of the wind. The air felt crisp, and everything seemed to hold its breath in anticipation. And then, as if on cue, the song "Perfect" began to play, its melody softly drifting through the stillness, filling the night with a warmth that matched the glow of the stars above.

She stood up suddenly, her eyes sparkling with excitement, and with a playful smile, she said, "Let's dance."

I was so lost in her presence, captivated by the magic of the moment, that I got up without even registering what she had said. But before I knew it, we were dancing. Our movements were natural, fluid, as though we had rehearsed them a thousand times.

She twirled around effortlessly, swinging from my hand, her laughter ringing through the night as we moved in perfect harmony. The road, the mountains, the stars — they all seemed to fade away, leaving just the two of us in our own world. Under the starlit sky, we swayed, completely absorbed in each other, the song wrapping around us like a soft embrace.

As she swung around, her hand still in mine, she came close—closer than ever before. Our bodies were just inches apart, and I could feel the warmth radiating from her as if we were the only sources of heat on that cold, misty night.

Naman Porwal

The space between us felt charged with electricity, our unspoken emotions crackling in the air. Her breath, warm and soft, grazed my skin, sending a shiver down my spine. Her lips hovered mere inches from mine, tantalizingly close but just out of reach.

I could see her eyes, those deep, mesmerizing eyes, filled with something unspoken. They seemed to be trying to tell me everything she had never said aloud. We both paused, frozen in the gravity of the moment, lost in the pull between us. Her soft vanilla scent engulfed me, drawing me in deeper. My heart pounded wildly in my chest, each beat echoing in my ears. And as I stood there, so close to her that I could feel her heart racing too, all I could think—what my soul was screaming—was "I love you."

For a fleeting moment, it felt like time had slowed, stretching those precious seconds into what felt like an eternity. The world around us faded into the background, leaving just the two of us standing there, on the edge of something we couldn't come back from. Then, as if we were being pulled by some invisible force stronger than either of us, we closed the gap between us.

Her lips met mine, soft and warm, and the world seemed to stop entirely. The kiss wasn't just a meeting of lips—it was a merging of souls, a silent confession of everything we had kept hidden inside. Her breath mingled with mine, our breaths becoming one, as if we were sharing the same air. Every heartbeat, every touch, every movement felt heightened, intense, as though our entire beings were pouring into that kiss. My hands instinctively moved to her waist, pulling her closer, and in that moment, it felt as if nothing else mattered.

In Her Eyes

Her lips were soft yet firm, delicate but with a passion that matched the fire inside me. Each movement of our lips felt like a silent promise, a conversation without words, as if we had been waiting for this moment for so long. I could feel the urgency in her kiss, the need to be close, to be connected. The heat between us grew, and with every breath we shared, I felt more alive than I ever had before.

Her fingers traced the line of my jaw, sending sparks across my skin, and I deepened the kiss, savouring every second, every sensation. Our hearts, once racing separately, now seemed to beat in perfect sync, a rhythm only we could hear. It was as though the rest of the world had faded away, leaving just the two of us, lost in each other's arms, in the embrace of the moment we had both been waiting for.

And as our lips parted, the world around us seemed to come back into focus, the beauty of the Swiss Alps stretching out before us once more. But in that moment, all that mattered was the love that burned between us, a flame that could never be extinguished.

We drove deeper into the heart of the Swiss Alps, a sense of serenity washed over us, the quiet hum of the car mingling with the gentle rustle of the wind. We didn't need words to express what we were feeling. The lingering warmth of our kiss spoke volumes, binding us together in a silent embrace of love and longing.

With her hand nestled securely in mine, I navigated the winding mountain roads with ease. We arrived at our destination at dawn and it was still few hours before sunrise.

Together, we embarked on a journey to the summit, our footsteps echoing in the stillness of the morning. As we reached the peak, we found a secluded spot to watch the sunrise, our hearts beating in time with the rhythm of nature unfolding before us.

In the quiet stillness of the mountain peak, with the first light of dawn painting the sky in soft pastel hues, we sat side by side, our fingers intertwined in a silent affirmation of our connection. The chill of the morning air was chased away by the warmth of our entwined hands, a tangible reminder of the bond that held us together.

As she leaned her head against my shoulder, her presence felt like a gentle caress against my skin, filling me with a sense of peace and contentment. I wrapped my arm around her shoulders, pulling her close, wanting to hold onto this moment forever.

Together, we watched as the sun slowly climbed higher in the sky, its golden rays illuminating the landscape with a radiant glow. And in that quiet embrace, surrounded by the majesty of the Swiss Alps, I knew that I had found my home—in her arms, under the open sky, with the promise of a new day stretching out before us.

"What do you think it's like at the top of that mountain?" she asked, gazing at the peak.

I smiled. "Let's go find out."

We trekked to the top of the mountain that had intrigued Stella. The path was blanketed in pure white snow, the world around us silent except for the soft crunch beneath our boots. The air was crisp, carrying a sense of adventure as we moved through the stillness, surrounded by snow-laden trees and slopes. As we climbed higher, I couldn't resist, scooping up a handful of snow and tossing it playfully at her.

In Her Eyes

She gasped in surprise before breaking into a laugh, her eyes sparkling as she retaliated with her own handful of snow. "Noah!" she exclaimed, her voice filled with warmth and excitement. We exchanged more playful snow throws, our laughter echoing through the quiet wilderness, the cold air filling with our joy.

As we caught our breath, she looked at me, her cheeks flushed from the cold and the laughter. "Noah, you know… I feel alive when I'm with you," she said, her voice soft but filled with sincerity.

I smiled at her, my heart swelling at her words. "And I get lost when I'm with you, Stella. Lost in you."

We continued our trek, hand in hand, the warmth of her touch grounding me in a way I had only dreamed about. It was exactly like the dreams I'd had—walking side by side, together, as if nothing else in the world mattered. The silence between us was comfortable, filled with the unspoken connection we shared, as if the mountain itself was bearing witness to something extraordinary between us.

When we finally reached the peak, the sight before us took our breath away. Below, tiny houses were nestled in the valley, their roofs completely covered in snow, making them look like little white dots scattered across a vast blanket of white. The entire landscape was a sea of snow, stretching endlessly in every direction. The sky above was pale, a soft blue blending into the horizon.

Stella squeezed my hand, her eyes wide with wonder. "It's beautiful," she whispered, her voice barely above a breath.

"It is," I replied, but my gaze wasn't on the view—it was on her. The way her eyes lit up, the way she seemed to belong in this moment, in this place. She was the most beautiful thing in the world to me. And as we stood there, taking in the breathtaking view, I realized that this—her, us—was everything I had ever wanted.

As we stood at the peak, surrounded by the vast, snowy landscape, Stella turned to me, her eyes filled with awe. "I hope I could stay here," she whispered, her voice carried softly by the cool mountain breeze.

Without missing a beat, I responded, "Let's do it."

She looked at me in surprise, her brows raising in disbelief. "What?" she asked, a mix of excitement and curiosity creeping into her voice.

I smiled, watching the way her expression shifted from disbelief to excitement. "There are camps nearby," I explained. "We can stay here, under the stars, just the two of us."

Her face lit up like the morning sun. "Are you serious?" she asked, her eyes sparkling with joy.

I nodded, unable to contain my smile as I saw how much the idea thrilled her. She had this way of lighting up, like a little kid on Christmas morning, and seeing her like that filled me with a warmth I couldn't quite put into words. It was infectious, and I could feel my own excitement growing just by looking at her.

"I can't believe it!" she exclaimed, practically bouncing with excitement. "This is going to be amazing!"

I chuckled, watching her joy spill out so freely. "I know it will be."

In Her Eyes

As we stood there, the world blanketed in snow around us, her excitement made the moment feel even more magical. This place, this moment—it was perfect. And the thought of spending the night here, under the stars, with her by my side, made my heart race. I was already looking forward to every second of it.

We descended from the peak, the snow crunching beneath our boots as we made our way down the familiar path, excitement lingering in the air between us. The camps we had passed earlier now beckoned, a perfect hideaway nestled amidst the towering trees and serene mountains. When we reached the site, we quickly put our backpacks inside the tents, our temporary home for the night.

As the evening unfolded, we found ourselves sitting near a gentle river, its soft gurgling blending harmoniously with the crackle of a bonfire. The warmth of the flames provided a cozy contrast to the cold mountain air, and the flickering light cast playful shadows on Stella's face, making her look even more radiant.

We met some fellow travelers, sharing stories and laughter, their company adding to the magic of the night. The soft strumming of a guitar accompanied by soothing music filled the atmosphere, creating a peaceful rhythm that made everything feel just right. But amidst it all, the most comforting presence was Stella, sitting beside me, her hand brushing against mine every so often, grounding me in the moment.

After a few hours, the others started retreating to their tents, the camp growing quieter as the night deepened. But we stayed. We sat by the fire, our eyes drawn upward to the vast, star-strewn sky. The stars above were brighter than I had ever seen, twinkling like diamonds against the inky blackness.

"It's beautiful," she whispered, her voice barely audible over the crackle of the fire and the gentle rush of the river.

I glanced at her, seeing the awe in her eyes as she gazed at the stars. "Yeah," I replied softly, though my gaze wasn't on the sky. It was on her. "It really is."

There was something so perfect about that moment—sitting with her under the vast, glittering sky, the world quiet and still, as if time itself had paused to let us breathe, to let us exist in this perfect space between the earth and the stars.

We crawled into the small, cozy tent, its canvas walls pressing in close around us, creating an intimate space where the world outside seemed distant. The cold mountain air lingered outside, but inside, the warmth between us made it feel comforting. We laid down, and the proximity of the space meant we were already close, our shoulders brushing against each other.

As the night wore on, I could feel Stella shifting in her half-asleep state. Without thinking, she moved closer, her body instinctively seeking warmth and comfort. In that moment, I gently offered her my shoulder, my arm wrapping around her as she nestled against my chest.

The sensation of her head resting on me, her soft breaths warming my skin, filled me with a sense of calm I hadn't felt in a long time. I could feel her chest rise and fall with each breath, her closeness a soothing rhythm against my own. Her scent—delicate and familiar—wrapped around me, lulling me into a peaceful state of contentment.

In Her Eyes

The night outside was still, the occasional rustle of the wind through the trees, but inside that tent, it felt like time had stopped. I found myself staring at her, the gentle rise and fall of her chest, the way her face softened in sleep. With her so near, her warmth enveloping me, I felt my own breathing slow, my thoughts quiet. I drifted into sleep with the comforting knowledge that she was there, beside me, as close as she could possibly be. It was the most peaceful sleep I had had in a long time, knowing that in that moment, everything was perfect.

Naman Porwal

5. When life takes a turn

We slipped back into the familiar routine of college life, yet everything felt a little different now. Each day, we'd meet up after our classes, sitting in our usual spot in the library or on her apartment roof or cafe. It became a ritual, sharing stories about our day—lectures, assignments, random moments that made us laugh or sigh.

But in between those conversations, there were stolen moments. A quick glance in a crowded hallway where our eyes met, holding each other's gaze a little too long. Sometimes, in the midst of our talks, her hand would find mine, and we'd sit there, fingers entwined, not needing to say anything. Those small gestures felt like our secret, a quiet acknowledgment of the bond that had deepened between us.

Occasionally, we'd sneak away after class to spend time alone. A walk through the park, an impromptu coffee stop, or just sitting together in silence, content in each other's company. There was a sweetness in those moments, brief but meaningful, where time seemed to stretch and everything else melted away.

One day at the college campus, I found myself standing at the base of the stairs, gazing up towards the first floor where Stella stood. She was watching me, her eyes locked onto mine, and for a brief moment, the world around us seemed to fade away. She looked stunning, her beauty catching me off guard, and I could feel my heart quicken as I became completely lost in her gaze. There was something in the way she looked back, as if she too was caught in the same spell.

It was as if time had slowed, both of us suspended in that shared moment, unaware of anything else. But then, suddenly, the magic shattered. As Stella began to descend the stairs, her focus still on me, she mis-stepped. I saw her body tilt, her balance falter, and before I could even process what was happening, she slipped, tumbling down the staircase.

"Stella!" I shouted, panic surging through my chest. I ran towards her, my legs moving as fast as they could, but it all happened so quickly. In an instant, she was on the ground at the bottom of the stairs, her body crumpled from the fall. I froze for a heartbeat, my stomach twisting in fear as I saw the blood—on her head, her legs, and scratches covering her hands.

I rushed to her side, my hands trembling as I called for an ambulance. My voice was shaking as I relayed the details, my eyes never leaving Stella, who lay unconscious on the cold floor. Time stretched unbearably as we waited for help to arrive.

When the ambulance finally pulled up, I helped them lift her onto the stretcher, my heart racing as I climbed in beside her. I could barely breathe, my mind reeling from the sight of her injuries. I grasped her hand tightly, my voice shaky as I whispered, "Hold on, Stella... please, just hold on."

As the ambulance sped through the streets, the sirens blaring, I felt a heavy weight pressing down on my chest. I couldn't bear the thought of losing her, not like this, not now.

As I sat in the waiting area outside the hospital room, my mind raced with dark thoughts. Every possible worst-case scenario flashed through my head. What if she didn't wake up? What if she was seriously injured? My heart pounded in my chest, my body tense as I anxiously waited for any news. The sterile hospital walls seemed to close in on me, each second feeling like an eternity.

Finally, after what felt like an endless 30 minutes, the door to the room opened. A doctor stepped out, his expression calm. My heart jumped into my throat as I stood up, bracing myself for the worst.

"Don't worry," the doctor said, his voice steady, instantly soothing some of my fear. "She's going to be fine."

Relief washed over me like a tidal wave. I felt the tension in my shoulders release, my breath coming out in a shaky exhale. The doctor explained that Stella had some scratches on her hands, but the more serious injury was to her legs. "She'll need to rest her legs for 10 to 15 days," he continued, "and she shouldn't put any pressure on them during that time."

I nodded, absorbing his words. I was just grateful she was okay. Knowing that the worst was behind us, a sense of relief flooded me. I thanked the doctor, feeling like I could finally breathe again. All that mattered now was that she was safe.

I knew I wasn't great at driving, but for Stella, I had to learn. I brought my car, the one I'd barely ever used, and picked her up from her apartment. She was hesitant at first, still adjusting to being in a wheelchair, but I reassured her with a soft smile. "Don't worry, I've got you," I said, gently lifting her into the car.

Each day, I spent my time with her, taking her to all her classes. I pushed her wheelchair across the campus, navigating through the crowded hallways and courtyards. People started to notice. They'd glance at us, whispering to one another. I could feel their eyes, but it didn't matter. All I cared about was making sure Stella was comfortable, cared for, and happy.

Between lectures, I'd sit with her, joking about the professors or discussing assignments. And after classes, I'd take her back to her apartment. I'd make sure she got inside safely, that she had everything she needed. Every night, I brought her food and stayed with her until she was settled into bed. Only then would I leave, often late into the night, feeling a strange comfort in the routine.

One evening, as I was helping Stella into her apartment, I saw Elena standing nearby, watching us. Her eyes followed my every move as I carefully wheeled Stella inside. Elena had warned me before about getting too close, but now, seeing me dedicate so much time and care to Stella, she looked different—softer, like she finally understood how deep my feelings ran.

Despite everything, I couldn't imagine being anywhere else. Taking care of Stella felt right, even if she isn't with me.

Naman Porwal

This was love for me: being there, no matter what, and giving everything without expecting anything in return.

The rain had become a quiet, constant companion, drizzling softly as the days passed. It was always there, like the unspoken emotions between Stella and me—gentle but persistent, never truly leaving. Every morning, as I drove to her apartment, the world outside the window was misty, drops of rain clinging to the glass as if mirroring the uncertainty that still lingered in the air between us.

Stella had grown used to the routine of me picking her up. She would greet me with a soft smile, and we would drive in comfortable silence to campus, the sound of rain tapping against the roof of the car. I'd wheel her from class to class, and though we talked and laughed about small things, there was an unspoken tension, a quiet question hanging between us that neither of us dared to answer.

One day, as I pushed her through the wet cobblestone paths of the university, the rain heavier than usual, Stella suddenly reached out and touched my hand. I stopped, feeling the cold air brush against my skin as I turned to her.

"Noah," she began, her voice soft, almost drowned out by the rain. "Why are you doing this? You don't have to take care of me every day."

I paused, searching for the right words as the raindrops continued to fall around us, creating a soft mist that blurred the world. "Then who would take care of you?" I finally said. "I don't do this out of obligation, Stella. I do it because I care about you."

Her eyes softened, and for a moment, she seemed on the verge of saying something more. But then she looked away,

In Her Eyes

glancing at the damp world around us. "It's just... you're always here. You've been so good to me, but..."

The sentence trailed off, swallowed by the rain. I swallowed hard, feeling a familiar knot form in my chest. "But what?"

She hesitated, biting her lip as if unsure whether to continue. "I don't want you to feel like you're stuck, Noah. You have your own life, and I don't want to be the reason you put it on hold."

The wind rustled through the trees, sending droplets cascading down around us. I crouched down to her level, the rain soaking through my jacket, but I didn't care. "I'm not stuck," I said, my voice firm but tender. "You've been hurt, Stella. I'm here because I want to be. And if that means helping you get through this, then that's what I'll do."

For a long moment, we stayed like that, the mist swirling around us, the sound of rain falling in the background. Her eyes searched mine, as if looking for something, and I held her gaze, hoping she'd see the sincerity in my words.

Then, without warning, she sighed and leaned back into her wheelchair, her eyes glistening. "I don't deserve this," she whispered. "I don't deserve you."

The weight of her words hit me harder than I expected. I stood up, gripping the handles of the wheelchair, unsure how to respond. The rain continued to fall, the drops streaking down her face like tears.

"You don't have to deserve anything," I finally said. "I'm not doing this because of what you deserve. I'm doing it because I love you."

Naman Porwal

Stella looked at me, her expression unreadable, and for a moment, I thought I saw something flicker in her eyes—regret, maybe, or sadness. But she said nothing, just turned her gaze back to the rain-soaked campus ahead.

We continued on in silence, the mist hanging heavy around us, the wet weather wrapping everything in a quiet, melancholic haze. After classes ended, I wheeled her back to the apartment as usual. But when we arrived, instead of letting me help her inside, she stopped me at the door. "Noah, you should go. I can manage from here."

I frowned, unsure of what had changed. "Are you sure? I don't mind helping—"

"I'm sure," she interrupted, her voice firm but gentle. "Thank you, for everything. But I need to be alone tonight."

I stared at her, my heart sinking, but I nodded. "Okay. Call me if you need anything."

She didn't respond, just gave me a small, tired smile before wheeling herself inside. The door clicked shut behind her, leaving me standing there in the rain, the cold droplets mixing with the unease building inside me. I walked back to my car, the wet pavement gleaming under the streetlights, the rain falling heavier now. As I sat in the driver's seat, I stared at the apartment building, wondering what had shifted between us.

The rain drummed against the windshield, relentless and unforgiving, just like the thoughts swirling in my mind. I started the car, driving slowly through the misty streets and mountains, feeling the weight of the night pressing down on me.

I had been doing everything I could to show her how much I cared, to be there for her. But maybe, just maybe, I was losing her anyway.

The rain had lessened to a fine drizzle, mist rising from the ground and creating a soft haze as I pulled up in front of Stella's apartment. I had come to pick her up like I had done every day for the past few weeks. But today, something felt different.

When she opened the door, she was standing on her own. No crutches, no wheelchair, just her, balanced and upright. For a moment, I stood there, frozen in place, the sight of her standing catching me off guard. The drizzle glistened in her hair, and her expression was unreadable as she sat in the car.

"I can walk on my own now, Noah," she said softly, her voice carrying over the sound of the gentle rain. "You don't have to pick me up anymore. You don't have to walk me around the campus. I'll be okay."

Her words hit me with a strange finality. It wasn't just about her physical recovery; there was something deeper, something unsaid between the lines. I could feel it in the way she avoided my eyes, the way her voice trembled ever so slightly.

"I didn't do it because I had to, Stella," I replied, stepping closer to her, the rain dampening my jacket. "I did it because I wanted to. I never felt embarrassed. Not once."

We reached campus and got out of car. She said with a sad smile flickering across her face. "Noah, you've been amazing. You've been there for me when I needed you the most. But now I can take care of myself. You don't have to feel obligated anymore."

Naman Porwal

I blinked, feeling a knot tighten in my chest. "Obligated? Is that what you think this is about?"

Her eyes met mine then, rain softly falling between us, and for the first time, I saw the weight of everything she had been holding in. "I don't want you to feel like you're stuck with me," she said, her voice breaking slightly. "I don't want to be the reason you hold back."

I stepped forward, closing the gap between us. "Stella, I'm not stuck. You have no idea how much I—" I stopped, catching my breath as my emotions welled up. "I care about you more than you think. This isn't about obligation or feeling embarrassed. I've never once felt that way."

She looked down at the ground, the rain falling in delicate drops, and let out a soft sigh. "It's just... I need to stand on my own again. And you—Noah, you need to live your life without feeling like you have to take care of me."

The words hung in the air between us, mingling with the mist and the rain that blurred the world around us. I opened my mouth to argue, to tell her how wrong she was, how I didn't mind, how I wanted to be there for her, always. But something in her expression stopped me. This wasn't just about walking again. It was about reclaiming her independence, about finding her own strength.

I nodded slowly, swallowing the lump in my throat. "I understand."

She looked at me with those eyes that had always been a mystery to me—soft, distant, yet filled with an emotion I couldn't quite place. "Thank you, Noah," she said, her voice barely above a whisper. "For everything."

She turned and walked towards campus, each step she took sending ripples of uncertainty through me. I watched her go, the rain casting a soft glow around her as she disappeared into the misty distance.

And just like that, she was gone. Walking on her own, no longer needing me to carry her through the day. As I stood there, alone in the rain, I couldn't help but wonder if that meant she didn't need me at all anymore. Watching her walk away, I felt the weight of the rain, the mist clinging to everything around me as if echoing the uncertainty now between us. I wanted to reach out, to call her back, to say something that would fix the growing distance.

But I didn't.

Instead, I stood there, letting the soft rain blur the edges of everything. The wet weather seemed to perfectly mirror the storm inside me—a mix of emotions I couldn't fully understand. I thought about all the time we had spent together, the care, the effort. It was hard to accept that she wanted to walk her own path now, even though I had been by her side through it all.

As I finally turned and walked back to my car, I realized that maybe, for the first time, I had to learn to walk away too.

Amidst the wet air and misty mornings, a sense of unease lingered in the back of my mind, a nagging doubt that refused to be ignored. I couldn't shake it off, no matter how hard I tried. And then, one day, Mike pulled me aside, his expression grim, his eyes filled with something more than concern.

"Noah, I need to talk to you," he began, his voice low and urgent, cutting through the damp air. The way he

Naman Porwal

looked at me made my heart sink. "I know you care about Stella, but you need to be careful. She's just using you, man. She's still in a relationship with Paul."

His words hit me like a punch to the gut, the reality crashing down around me with a force that left me breathless. The rain outside was steady, drumming against the window like a cruel reminder of the uncertainty flooding my mind. I stared at Mike, trying to process what he had said, but I struggled to believe it.

"No," I said, shaking my head slowly, my voice barely above a whisper. "It's not like that. She's... she wouldn't do that."

Mike's gaze didn't waver. "I'm telling you this because I care about you man. You're giving her everything, and she's still with Paul. I've seen her texting him."

A knot of frustration tightened in my chest, but I pushed it aside. "Mike, you don't understand. She's going through a lot. I don't want to give up on her."

Even as I spoke the words, doubt gnawed at me, but I clung to the hope that Mike was wrong. Ignoring his warning, I brushed off his concerns and continued to pour my heart into my friendship with Stella. I kept telling myself I could prove him wrong, that she cared about me the way I cared about her.

But as the days passed, my unease only grew stronger, fueled by the sight of Stella constantly on her phone. I'd catch glimpses of her smiling softly at the screen, her attention split between me and whoever was on the other end of the line. I tried not to care. I tried to convince myself it was nothing, that everything would fall into place. But the doubt, like the endless rain outside, refused to let up.

In Her Eyes

And with each passing day, I wondered if Mike's words had more truth than I was willing to admit.

Elena approached me one evening as I came out of my apartment, her face clouded with concern, and as the misty drizzle fell softly around us, her urgency was palpable. The rain lightly dotted her hair and jacket, but she didn't seem to notice—her focus was entirely on me.

"Noah, you need to listen to me," she said, her voice firm yet gentle, cutting through the damp air like a blade. Her eyes held mine with a serious intensity that made my heart skip. "Stella is not good for you. She's playing games, Noah. You need to stay away from her before you get hurt again."

Her words hit me harder than I expected, each syllable heavy with the weight of truth. I felt the sting of her warning settle over me, like the cold rain soaking into my skin. My chest tightened, and I found myself unable to meet her gaze for a moment, staring instead at the wet pavement beneath our feet.

"Elena, you don't understand..." I began, my voice weak, but she interrupted me, shaking her head.

"I understand more than you think, Noah," she said, stepping closer, her eyes soft with concern. "I see what's happening. Stella is keeping you on the edge, stringing you along while she's still wrapped up in her own world. You're giving her everything, and she's giving you nothing but heartache. I don't want to see you go through this again."

I wanted to believe Elena was wrong, but deep down, I knew her words were true. I'd seen it too—Stella's distant stares, the unanswered texts, the way she disappeared into her own thoughts when I was right next to her.

Naman Porwal

The rain picked up, and the air grew colder as I stood there, feeling the ache of reality finally sinking in. Elena's gaze softened, her voice more gentle now. "You need to let go of this fantasy, Noah. I know it's hard, but you're only going to get hurt more if you keep holding on. It's time to face the truth."

I looked up, meeting her eyes, and in that moment, I knew she was right. The fantasy I had clung to—the hope that Stella would choose me, that she would see me the way I saw her—was just that.

The cold rain washed over us, blurring the world around me, but as I stood there with Elena's words echoing in my mind, I felt a quiet resolve take root in my heart. It was time to let go and face the truth head-on, no matter how much it hurt.

In Her Eyes

6. No turning back

As Stella and I trekked through the mist-laden forest in a chilly November, the air was thick with the fresh scent of pine and earth, while a light drizzle fell steadily around us, softening the sounds of our footsteps on the damp leaves beneath. The gentle murmur of a nearby stream echoed in the background, blending seamlessly with the rustle of wind through the trees. It felt like we had stepped into another world, one cloaked in mist and the quiet embrace of nature.

"So, Noah, what do you think life is all about?" Stella asked, her voice thoughtful and curious as she glanced up at me from beneath the dripping canopy of branches. The mist curled around her, softening the edges of everything around us, turning her into an ethereal figure.

I smiled, feeling a warmth bloom in my chest despite the chill in the air. "I think life is about finding happiness in the little things," I said, my voice calm and steady as my gaze drifted over the verdant landscape shrouded in mist. The droplets of rain shimmered on the leaves like diamonds. "Moments like this—where it's just us, surrounded by nature, with nothing but the sound of rain and the quiet rhythm of the forest. It's peaceful."

Stella nodded, her lips curling into a smile as her eyes sparkled, catching the faint light breaking through the overcast sky. She reached down and gently plucked a small wildflower, its fragile petals beaded with rain. "There's something truly magical about being here," she murmured, twirling the flower between her fingers. "Away from the noise and chaos of the city, it's like... we can breathe."

We paused for a moment, standing still as the mist swirled around us, the forest humming with life. I glanced at her, feeling the connection between us deepen in the tranquility of the moment. The soft rain fell in a rhythm as gentle as our conversation, wrapping the world in a comforting veil of silence. The beauty of the forest, the mist, and the rain made everything feel timeless.

"Yeah," I whispered, the words carried on the cool breeze. "Out here, it feels like everything else disappears."

As we reached the edge of the river and settled down on the banks, the soothing sound of rushing water filling the air around us, I couldn't help but feel a sense of peace wash over me. And as I gazed at the beauty of the natural world around us, my eyes inevitably drifted to Stella, her presence a beacon of light in the darkness of my soul.

"What are you looking at?" she asked, her voice breaking through the quiet serenity of the moment.

Still facing her, my heart pounding in my chest as I struggled to find the words to say.

"The absolute beauty," I said smiling, still looking at her.

"And what's that," she asked teasingly.

In Her Eyes

"You, Stella," I confessed, my voice barely above a whisper. "You're the most beautiful thing happened to me."

A soft smile tugged at the corners of her lips as she met my gaze, her eyes shimmering with warmth and affection. "Thank you, Noah," she replied, her voice soft and gentle. "Thanks for always being there for me."

But as the moment stretched on, the weight of my unspoken words pressing down upon me like a heavy burden, I knew that I could no longer hide the truth from her. With a heavy heart, I took a deep breath and finally spoke the words that had been weighing on my soul for far too long.

"Stella, I... I can't do this anymore," I began, my voice trembling with emotion as I met her gaze with a mixture of sadness and resignation. "I can't be just friends with you. I've tried, but... but I still love you, Stella. And I can't bear the thought of pretending otherwise."

A flicker of confusion passed across her features, her eyes searching mine for any sign of clarity. "Noah, what are you saying?" she asked, her voice tinged with uncertainty.

I swallowed hard, I struggled to find the courage to speak the truth. "I'm saying that it's better if you leave me alone, Stella," I replied, my voice hoarse with emotion. "I can't keep pretending that everything is okay when it's not. I need to let you go, for both of our sakes."

And as the weight of my words hung in the air between us, the silence stretching on like an eternity, I couldn't help but feel a sense of sadness wash over me. For in that moment, I knew that I had lost not only a friend, but a piece of my heart as well.

Naman Porwal

As the words hung heavy in the air between us, the tension palpable and thick with unspoken emotions, Stella's voice broke through the silence like a thunderclap, her tone laced with confusion and disbelief.

"Where is this coming from, Noah?" she demanded, her eyes narrowing in frustration as she turned to face me, her expression a mixture of anger and hurt.

"It's always been there, Stella," I replied, my voice barely above a whisper as I met her gaze with a mixture of sadness and resignation.

Her brow furrowed in confusion, her eyes searching mine for any sign of clarity. "What do you mean, it's always been there?" she asked, her voice tinged with uncertainty. "Why can't we just be friends?" she continued, her tone pleading as she reached out to touch my arm in a gesture of comfort. "I don't understand, Noah. We've been through so much together. Why does it have to end like this?"

But as she spoke, her words only served to deepen the chasm between us, the gulf of misunderstanding widening with each passing moment. And as I struggled to find the courage to speak my truth, I knew that there could be no turning back from the path that lay before us.

"You still talk to Paul, don't you?" I asked, my voice trembling with emotion as I met her gaze.

Stella's face reddened with anger, her eyes flashing with indignation as she recoiled from my accusation. "So, what if I talk to him?" she demanded, her voice rising with each word. "Why should it bother you, Noah?"

But even as she spoke, I could see the guilt and shame flickering behind her eyes, the truth of her words ringing hollow in the face of the undeniable evidence before us. And as the weight of her betrayal settled over me like a heavy blanket, I couldn't help but feel a sense of despair wash over me, knowing that our friendship had been built on a foundation of lies and deceit.

With a heavy heart, my eyes burning with unshed tears, I struggled to contain the flood of emotions threatening to consume me. I knew that there could be no going back from this moment of reckoning.

"I know now, Noah," Stella said, her voice tinged with bitterness as she met my gaze with a mixture of anger and hurt. "I know where this is coming from. Mike and Elena have been filling your ears with poison, haven't they? They're the ones turning you against me. They talk to you but don't talk to me."

"You're the one who pushed them away, Stella," I replied, my voice tinged with frustration. "You're the one who keep yourself distant, who talks to Paul or whoever instead of being present with your friends. And now you want to blame them for our problems?"

Stella's expression softened, a flicker of uncertainty passing across her features as she met my gaze with a mixture of sadness and regret. "Noah, it's not like that," she protested, her voice pleading for understanding. "I don't talk to Paul, it's John. And there's nothing going on between us, I swear."

"I don't know whom you talk to, Stella," I continued, my voice trembling with emotions. "But when I see you online and wait for hours, knowing that you're still there but choosing not to reply to my messages or take my calls, it hurts. Stella, it hurts more than you can imagine."

A pang of guilt stabbed at my heart as I watched her struggle to find the right words to say, the weight of my accusations hanging heavy in the air between us like a shroud of darkness. But even as I fought to contain the flood of emotions threatening to consume me, I knew that I couldn't keep silent any longer, couldn't continue to pretend that everything was okay when it wasn't.

"I've tried to give you space, to tolerate your behavior and accept that there are others in your life," I admitted, my voice barely above a whisper as I struggled to contain the flood of emotions threatening to overwhelm me. "But you don't realize how your actions make me feel, Stella. You don't see the pain and the jealousy that I've been forced to endure, all because you can't be bothered to give me the time I deserve."

"I don't know if I can trust you, Stella," I said, my voice trembling, barely audible as I met her gaze. "I don't know who you're talking to, who you're spending your time with. You've shut me out of your life, and I don't know if I can live with that."

As the weight of my words hung in the air, a sudden downpour began, the rain falling in heavy sheets, soaking us within moments. The droplets mixed with the tears that welled in my eyes, making it impossible for her to see the pain etched in my expression. I blinked against the rain, my heart aching, but my emotions stayed hidden beneath the storm's veil.

Stella stood silently in front of me, her hair plastered to her face, her lips parted as if searching for something to say. But the rain fell harder, drowning out everything except the quiet sound of her breathing. The storm mirrored the turmoil between us—unforgiving, relentless.

In Her Eyes

And as the silence stretched on like an eternity, the reality of our broken bond became inescapable. The lies and the distance that had crept between us had shattered what we once had. Despite the cold rain chilling my skin, I could only feel the sadness settling deeper, a quiet resignation that washed over me like the rain itself.

The thunder rumbled faintly in the distance, but neither of us moved. The storm outside was nothing compared to the one swirling in my chest.

As we drove away from the forest, the steady hum of the car drowned out the storm of emotions churning inside me. We sat in silence, the weight of unspoken words hanging heavily between us, though she sat just inches away.

Her eyes, brimming with tears and laced with a quiet anger, pierced through the darkness, cutting into me with a raw intensity that made me feel utterly exposed. Each glance from her felt like a wound, deepening the sense of despair that washed over me. I knew then, with a sinking heart, that I had caused her more pain than I could ever take back.

But even as I fought to contain the flood of emotions threatening to overwhelm me, a part of me knew that there could be no going back from this moment of reckoning, no undoing the damage that had been done.

As the days turned into weeks, and the weeks into months, I found myself drifting further and further away from Stella, the wounds of our past still raw and unhealed, festering beneath the surface like a silent storm waiting to erupt.

Despite her attempts to reach out to me, to bridge the divide that had grown between us like a gaping chasm, I couldn't bring myself to let her back into my life. The pain of our last encounter still fresh in my mind, the wounds still too raw to bear, I chose instead to retreat into myself, to build walls around my heart and shut her out completely.

And as the months passed by in a blur of empty days and sleepless nights, I found myself consumed by a sense of anger and resentment, a burning desire to escape the suffocating grip of our shared past and forge a new path for myself, one free from the pain and heartache that had come to define our relationship.

It was then that I made the decision to leave college early, to seek out a new beginning far away from the memories that haunted me at every turn. And though the prospect of starting over in a new place filled me with a sense of trepidation and uncertainty, I knew deep down that it was the only way to truly move on from the pain of our past and find the peace and happiness that had eluded me for so long.

So, as I prepare to embark on this new chapter of my life, I do so with a sense of hope and determination, knowing that no matter what challenges lie ahead, I have the strength and resilience to face them head on, and to finally leave the ghosts of my past behind me once and for all.

As the news of my new job in campus spread, a sense of relief washed over me, knowing that I would soon be able to leave behind the memories of my tumultuous past and start anew in a place where the ghosts of my past held no sway.

The prospect of returning to my hometown, of being able to live with my aging parents and be there for them in their time of need, filled me with a sense of purpose and determination, knowing that I could finally repay them for all the sacrifices they had made for me over the years.

In Her Eyes

But even as I counted down the days until my departure, I knew that I still had to face the remaining 4 months of my time on campus, the constant reminders of Stella and the pain of our failed relationship a constant thorn in my side.

As the days passed and our paths continued to cross on campus, I found myself trapped in a whirlwind of conflicting emotions, torn between the love and happiness I felt in Stella's presence and the lingering doubts and insecurities that gnawed at the edges of my mind like a relentless storm.

Despite my best efforts to keep my distance, to bury my feelings beneath a facade of indifference, I couldn't deny the pull she still had over me, the way her mere presence could set my heart racing and my pulse quickening with a mixture of longing and desire.

But as much as I wanted to believe that there was still hope for us, that we could find a way to bridge the chasm that had grown between us and rediscover the spark we once shared, the painful thought remained that she has someone else in her life, the person that she talks to everyday.

And so, as I sat in the Finance class that day, watching her take her seat beside me with a sense of longing and regret, I couldn't help but feel a sense of resignation wash over me, knowing that no matter how much I wished things could be different, some things were simply not meant to be. I realized that I couldn't force her to love me, couldn't make her see how much I care about her.

As Stella settled into the seat beside me in the Finance class, her presence a bittersweet reminder of the past we had shared, I couldn't help but feel a surge of emotions wash over me, the desire to be with her.

Naman Porwal

As she spoke, her voice soft and gentle, filled with genuine concern for my well-being, "Noah, how have you been?"

I couldn't let her see the turmoil raging within me, couldn't let her know how much her presence still affected me.

And so, with a heavy heart, I forced myself to reply in a voice barely above a whisper, masking the pain and longing that simmered beneath the surface. "I'm okay, Stella," I said, my words betraying the truth of my feelings even as I tried to maintain a facade of indifference.

But she saw through my facade, saw the pain and sadness hidden behind my words, and her expression softened with understanding. "I know you're not okay," she said gently, her eyes searching mine for any sign of vulnerability. "I know you took the early placement to get away from me."

My heart clenched at her words, the weight of her accusation hanging heavy in the air between us. I wanted to protest, to deny the truth of her words, but I knew that it was futile. The truth was written plainly on my face, in the silent tears that threatened to spill from my eyes.

"It's not like that," I murmured, my voice barely audible in the empty classroom. "We all have to think about the future." But even as I spoke the words, I couldn't shake the nagging feeling that I was only fooling myself, that no matter how hard I tried to move on, I would always be haunted by the memory of her.

As the last echoes of the lecture faded away and the classroom emptied, leaving only Stella and me behind, a palpable tension hung in the air between us, thick with unspoken words and unresolved emotions.

Outside, the skies darkened and the sound of rain tapping against the windows filled the room, the gentle pitter-patter of droplets against glass window mingling with the soft hum of the air conditioning.

For a moment, neither of us spoke, the silence stretching between us like a chasm too vast to bridge. But then, as if compelled by some unseen force, Stella turned to me, her eyes searching mine for any sign of understanding.

Taking a deep breath, she reached out and took my hand in her, the warmth of her touch a soothing balm to my weary soul. And as we stood there together, two souls adrift in a sea of uncertainty, I knew that no matter what the future held, we would weather the storm together, united by the bond that had always drawn us back to each other, time and time again.

Stella's hand ignited a spark within my heart that I thought had long since been extinguished. In that fleeting moment, as our fingers intertwined, I felt the walls I had built around my emotions crumble, replaced by an overwhelming tide of love and longing that threatened to consume me.

"Let's go back to being friends, please?"

I felt her words tug at something deep inside me, but I couldn't muster a response. Instead, I remained silent, staring ahead as the weight of everything we had been through settled between us. Slowly, almost involuntarily, I gave a small nod, unsure if I truly meant it, or if I was simply too tired to say otherwise. The silence lingered, heavy and unresolved.

Naman Porwal

For despite the pain and heartache she had caused me, I couldn't deny the depth of my feelings for her, couldn't ignore the magnetic pull she exerted over my heart and soul. In her presence, even the darkest moments seemed to shine with a radiant light, and every hurtful word or action paled in comparison to the love and joy she brought into my life.

And as I gazed into her eyes, seeing the flicker of uncertainty and vulnerability hidden within their depths, I knew that I couldn't remain angry with her any longer. For she was the best thing that had ever happened to me, the one who had captured my heart in ways I never thought possible.

And as I held her hand in mine, feeling the warmth of her touch seep into my very soul, I knew that I couldn't imagine my life without her by my side.

For she was my heart, my soul, my everything.

In Her Eyes

7. Clouded departures

At my farewell party, the atmosphere was tense. Everyone was aware of the emotional rollercoaster I had been through, and while they were excited for my new chapter in Zermatt, they harbored their own silent judgments about Stella. Elena, Mike, and my flat mates had made it clear they didn't think inviting her was a good idea. Despite their warnings, I had done it anyway.

Stella arrived late. As soon as she walked in, the room fell silent for a brief moment, and the subtle shift in mood was impossible to ignore. Eyes followed her every move, filled with sympathy for me and subtle judgment towards her. She made her way through the crowd towards me, her expression composed, but I could feel the weight of the tension in the air.

"Congratulations, Noah," she said softly, offering me a small smile, one that didn't reach her eyes.

I thanked her, but even as we exchanged pleasantries, I could feel the emotional wall between us. Around us, the conversations resumed, but no one engaged with her. They avoided her, their eyes flitting back to me with a kind of silent pity. It was suffocating. The warmth I once felt between us had been replaced by an unspoken awkwardness, and every glance, every whisper only seemed to dig the knife in deeper. Stella felt it too.

As the night wore on, I noticed her slipping into the background, standing alone by the window. Her presence was a reminder of the broken pieces I had tried to mend. I could see it in the way she hugged herself, as if trying to protect herself from the coldness that had settled in the room.

It hurt to see her like that, knowing that the same people who had supported me were now the ones making her feel isolated.

As the night dragged on, Stella's frustration became more and more apparent. She stood apart from the crowd, her body language tense, her eyes flickering to the door as if searching for an escape. She hadn't touched a single plate of food, hadn't spoken to anyone after our brief conversation. Finally, she quietly slipped out of the apartment.

I noticed her absence almost immediately and instinctively ran after her, my heart pounding not just from the running but from the unspoken tension between us.

"Stella!" I called out, catching up to her as she made her way down the street. She turned slightly, but kept walking. "Why are you leaving so early?"

"It's nothing, Noah," she replied, her voice clipped, as if she were holding back something deeper.

In Her Eyes

Concern etched in my voice, I pressed on. "You didn't eat anything. What's going on? Talk to me."

She stopped walking but didn't turn around at first. Her shoulders were rigid, and I could sense the storm brewing beneath her calm exterior. "I don't feel like eating," she muttered.

"Tell me what happened," I asked again, gently, but persistently. Her silence spoke volumes, but I needed to hear her say it. After a few more moments of pushing, she finally turned to face me, her eyes flashing with a mixture of frustration and pain.

"Noah, you won," she said, her voice tainted with bitterness. "I lost."

"What are you talking about?" I asked, bewildered.

"All of my friends—those people inside—I introduced you to them, and now they're on your side. They sympathize with you, judge me, and pretend I don't exist. I've lost everything, Noah. I don't have anyone left."

I stood there, absorbing her words, feeling the weight of her anguish. "Stella," I began softly, "I didn't win anything. How could I win when I lost you?" My voice cracked slightly. "I never wanted anything but you. You pushed me away. You... you still talk to Paul even after you told me you broke up. Have you really broken up, or did you just lie to me?"

The question hung in the air between us like a blade waiting to drop. Stella stared at me, her expression unreadable, her silence answering more than her words ever could.

My heart clenched. I could feel the finality in the moment, like a door slowly creaking shut on everything we had once been. "Anyway," I said, my voice thick with emotion, "it's all over now. I'm leaving tomorrow, and I'm going far away from you."

She didn't say anything, her stubbornness a wall between us. I didn't push any further. I knew there was nothing more left to say.

I dropped her home, the ride quiet, the tension suffocating. Before she got out of the car, I stopped by a small place to pack some food for her. As she was about to leave, I handed it to her, my voice soft, almost pleading, "Please eat."

She took the bag silently, not meeting my eyes, and disappeared into the night.

Next day, I set off for Zermatt, leaving everything behind, but despite my efforts, Stella still lingered in my thoughts. As I drove, the vast landscapes of the Swiss countryside passed by, my mind was elsewhere, caught between the past and the unknown future.

My phone rang. It was her. I hesitated for a second before answering. Before I could even greet her, Stella's voice cut through the silence, sharp and accusatory.

"What you have done is not good, Noah! You have left me all alone. How am I supposed to get through the rest of the college without you? You owe me—everything you have is because of me! I made you who you are. You're nothing without me."

Her words hit like a punch in the gut. I gripped the steering wheel tightly, the anger building in my chest. I could

In Her Eyes

not let her continue tearing me down. Without another word, I hung up, my heart heavy and my mind clouded with frustration. I decided then and there not to reach out to her again.

As I arrived in Zermatt, I threw myself into my new job, trying to lose myself in routine. But no matter how busy I kept myself, Stella's voice echoed in my mind, her words refusing to let go.

I went to Zurich for the convocation, trying to keep myself composed, but the moment I stepped onto campus, everything felt heavier. The rain had just stopped, and the air was cool, damp, carrying that familiar smell of wet stone and earth. As I walked through the crowd, my heart raced, not because of the ceremony but because I knew I might see her.

And then, there she was. Stella. Standing just a few steps away, surrounded by familiar faces, yet she seemed distant, almost untouchable. Our eyes met for a fleeting second, but in that moment, it felt like the ground beneath me shifted. A sharp ache twisted in my chest, the kind that only comes when you see someone who once meant everything. I could still see the traces of who we used to be in her eyes, but there was something different now—something broken, and I wasn't sure if it was her or me.

I looked away, trying to steady my breath as I made my way toward Elena and Mike. They greeted me with warm smiles, but I could tell by their eyes that they sensed the tension.

"How have you been, Noah?" Elena asked gently, her concern evident.

I forced a smile, feeling the weight of my emotions creeping in. "I've been... okay," I replied, though it felt like a lie. Mike patted me on the back, offering silent support. The conversation drifted to work, life, and everything in between, but my mind kept drifting back to Stella.

The heartache lingered, as though seeing her after all this time had reopened old wounds. I didn't know how to feel—whether it was regret or longing, but it was there, and I couldn't shake it.

As soon as I returned to my small apartment in Zermatt after the convocation in Zurich, I felt like I was suffocating. The rain had started again, softly tapping against the window, a cold and relentless reminder of the heaviness in my chest. I sat by the window, watching the raindrops race down the glass, their path mirroring the confusion and chaos in my mind.

I leaned my forehead against the cool windowpane, the fog from my breath creating a blurry haze. "Why do I still feel like this?" I whispered to myself, my voice barely audible over the sound of the rain. I could still see her, standing across the hall at the convocation. Our eyes met for just a fleeting second, but it was enough. Enough to reopen every wound, every unspoken word, every unfinished moment between us.

"Stella..." I muttered, as if saying her name would somehow summon an answer. I closed my eyes and, just like that, I got flooded with memories of her—her laugh, her scent, the way she used to lean her head on my shoulder when we were lost in our own world. All the nights we spent talking about our dreams, all the stolen moments, the kisses, the touch of her hand in mine. It all came rushing back like a tidal wave, and I wasn't sure if I could take it.

In Her Eyes

The panic started to build inside me, gripping my chest in that familiar, unbearable way. I could feel my heartbeat racing, the air in the room suddenly feeling too thick to breathe. I clenched my fists, pressing them hard against the cold window frame, as if grounding myself to something tangible might calm the storm inside me.

"I should have just stayed away. Why did I go?" I whispered, my voice trembling. I tried to steady my breath, but the weight of her presence—her absence—was too much. My mind spiralled back to that moment, back to Zermatt when she called me after I left for the job. Her voice, her words still rang painfully in my ears.

"What you have done is not good... You have left me alone. You are nothing without me!" Her voice was sharp, almost accusing, and it cut deeper than I had ever admitted to anyone, even to myself.

I could feel my hand tightening around the armrest as I recalled how I hung up on her, how I shut her out after those words. But in truth, I never really shut her out—she was always there, in the quiet moments, in the gaps between conversations with other people, in the nights when I lay in bed staring at the ceiling. She was there, haunting me.

"Why do I still care?" I whispered to the empty room, the rain outside the only response I got. "Why do I still... love her?" The words slipped out, and once they did, there was no taking them back.

I was still in love with her. Every part of her was etched into my soul, and it killed me because I knew she wasn't mine anymore, maybe she never was.

I stood up abruptly, feeling like the walls of the room were closing in on me. The rain had picked up outside, heavy now, almost violent. I opened the window and let the cool, wet air hit my face. I needed to breathe. I needed to feel something other than the crushing weight of her memory.

The sound of the rain filled the silence, a constant, soothing rhythm that didn't match the chaos in my mind. I leaned out, letting the cold drops soak my face, my hair, my clothes. I wanted to feel numb, but instead, all I felt was the growing ache inside me, the longing for something I couldn't have.

I took a shaky breath, 'Stella... where did it all go wrong? Why... why couldn't we fix it?'

The rain didn't answer.

I ran my fingers through my wet hair, leaning against the window frame. I thought back to that day she walked out of the farewell party, how she looked at me with that anger and hurt in her eyes. "Noah, you won. I lost." Her voice echoed in my mind, sharp and bitter. She had blamed me for everything falling apart, but was it really my fault? Or was it both of us?

My heart clenched as I thought of how things used to be, how easy it was to fall for her, to love her. But now... now it was all broken, and I didn't know how to fix it. Maybe I couldn't. Maybe it was too late.

I wiped the rain from my face, or maybe they were tears, I couldn't tell anymore. "God, why can't I just forget her?" I muttered, my voice breaking.

But I knew the answer. I knew it, deep down. I couldn't forget her because I was still in love with her. Because part

In Her Eyes

of me still wanted her, still hoped for her, even after everything that happened. Even after all the pain.

I closed the window, the rain continuing to pour outside, mirroring the storm inside me. I sat back down, staring blankly out into the night. The world outside was dark, wet, and cold, just like the way I felt inside.

I leaned my head back, closing my eyes as the memories of Stella filled my mind. I knew I needed to move on, to let her go, but I didn't know how. All I knew was that, despite everything, I was still in love with her. And that realization was both my comfort and my curse.

8. Under the same sky

That night, around 2 a.m., my phone rang, the vibration jolting me awake. I stared at the screen for a moment, blinking against the dim glow of the clock. Stella. My heart skipped a beat, and before I could stop myself, I answered.

"Hello?" I said, my voice rough with sleep, but I kept my tone guarded, not wanting her to sense the whirlwind of emotions she always stirred in me.

"Noah, how are you?" Her voice was soft, almost fragile. There was a vulnerability there, but I couldn't let myself fall into it. I had to keep my distance, or at least try.

"I'm okay," I responded, my tone flat, trying to mask the storm inside me. "What do you want, Stella?"

There was a pause, and I could hear her breathe in, as if she was gathering the courage to speak. "Why are you talking to me like this?" she asked, her voice faltering. "Don't you feel like talking to me?"

I felt the tension rise inside me, a mix of anger and longing that I had been trying to suppress. "Stella," I began, my voice edged with frustration, "I either stay in or I'm out. I don't do things halfway, and I don't pursue things when they spiral out of control. You know that."

There was silence on the other end, and for a moment, I wondered if she'd hung up. Then, in a trembling voice, barely above a whisper, she said, "I really need to meet you, Noah. I want to see you."

Her voice—so fragile, so full of emotion—hit me like a wave. Every wall I had built crumbled. Despite everything, despite the pain and the mess between us, I still cared. I couldn't ignore that. My heart softened, and before I could stop myself, I sighed and agreed.

"Okay," I said, my resolve weakening. "Let's meet."

I told my family I was heading for a training session, but in reality, I was meeting Stella in Zurich. It felt like a secret, like something forbidden, but I couldn't resist. When I saw her, standing there, looking like she had during the days when we were together, a flood of emotions surged through me. I hadn't realized how deeply I had buried my feelings for her until that very moment. The walls I had so carefully built around my heart collapsed, and I let my guard down completely.

We roamed the cobblestone streets of Zurich, wandering through old cafés, reminiscing about everything we once had. It felt natural, like slipping back into an old routine. The familiarity, the easy laughter between us—it was intoxicating. By the time we checked into a hotel room, we had become completely wrapped up in each other again.

We slept together that night, not just physically, but emotionally. The distance that had grown between us over the years vanished, and for a moment, it felt like everything was falling back into place. I let myself believe that maybe, just maybe, we could go back to what we once were.

But then, the spell broke.

Her phone screen lit up. Paul. The name flashed before my eyes, and suddenly, the ground beneath me shifted. After everything… after all this time, it was Paul. A rush of anger and insecurity twisted inside me as she picked up the call right in front of me. I watched, silent, while she spoke to him in the same calm, casual tone she had once used with me.

I waited. Minutes stretched into an hour, then two. She talked to him as if I weren't even there. The longer it went on, the angrier I became, every word she exchanged with him feeling like a knife.

When she finally hung up, I couldn't hold it in anymore.

"Are you still talking to Paul? You never stopped, did you?" My voice came out harsh, a mix of hurt and accusation. I felt my hands clenching at my sides, trying to steady myself.

She sighed, rolling her eyes as if I was being unreasonable. "Noah, it's not what you think. We're just friends, that's all."

"Just friends?" I snapped, my anger boiling over. "While I'm sitting here waiting for you, you talk to him for two hours? If he's just a friend, why are you keeping him in your life when I'm the one standing in front of you?"

Her eyes flashed with frustration. "I won't explain this again, Noah. I'm tired of this. You don't trust me. Why did you come here if you're just going to accuse me?"

I felt the rage bubbling over, but even in my anger, I couldn't help myself. I pulled her close and kissed her. It was fierce, desperate, like we were both trying to drown out everything unsaid, every painful word that had come before.

She was burning with fever. I could feel the heat radiating from her, but I didn't think much of it then. I left soon after, my emotions tangled in a mess of love, anger, and regret.

By the time I returned home, Elena called. She sounded worried. "Noah, Stella's sick. She's got COVID."

My stomach dropped. The realization hit me like a ton of bricks—if she was sick, I might be too. And then, the fear for my parents set in. I couldn't help but blame myself for meeting her, for letting her back into my life even though I knew it would end like this.

A few months after everything, we had a reunion planned with Elena, Mike, and, of course, Stella. It felt strange, knowing we were all going to meet again after the whirlwind of emotions that had passed between us. Stella and I arrived early, as we wanted to spend some time together before everyone else got there. We wandered through the streets, browsing through shops, making small talk, but I could sense an undercurrent of tension building up.

When Mike and Elena landed at the airport, they called, letting us know they were waiting to be picked up. I turned to Stella, gently nudging her, "We should hurry up. Mike and Elena are waiting."

Naman Porwal

Her expression darkened, and she let out a sharp sigh. "Why do we have to hurry up for your friends, Noah? Do they always come first?"

I was taken aback by her sudden anger, but instead of arguing, I decided to leave it. "Come on, Stella, they're waiting," I said, heading towards the car.

She didn't move, her eyes flashing with resentment. "You always put them first. I'm here with you, and all you care about is picking them up."

I didn't respond. I walked to the car and started it, the engine roaring to life as I pulled away slowly. From the rearview mirror, I saw her running behind, catching up just as I stopped to let her in. She got into the car, slamming the door, and the argument spilled over in the confined space.

"You never listen to me," she muttered under her breath, her arms crossed tightly across her chest.

I kept my focus on the road, silent, gripping the steering wheel.

Her voice rose, sharp and cutting. "You always prioritize everyone else, never me! You're more concerned about your stupid friends than about me!"

Still, I stayed quiet. I could feel the heat rising inside me, but I didn't want to escalate things further. I let her words hit me like waves, washing over but not sinking in.

"You know, sometimes I wonder if your family even cares about you!" she blurted out, crossing a line I didn't expect her to.

In Her Eyes

My knuckles turned white as I gripped the wheel tighter. I wanted to say something—anything—but I bit my tongue, choosing silence over adding fuel to the fire.

We pulled up to the airport, and Mike and Elena got in, immediately sensing the tension. "Hey, everything alright?" Mike asked, looking between us.

I forced a smile, "Yeah, everything's fine."

Stella stayed silent, fuming. The drive to the hotel was quiet, the air thick with unsaid words and unresolved anger.

That evening, at the hotel, I finally snapped when she was still complaining. "Stella, just shut up. Let's get through tonight, and after that, we're done. No more of this. No more fighting, no more anything."

She looked at me, shocked and hurt. But she didn't respond. At dinner, we sat around the table with Mike and Elena, trying to act normal, but the weight of everything between us hung over the meal like a dark cloud.

At one point, Stella reached out to hold my hand, her fingers brushing against mine. I pulled my hand away quickly, my voice low and cold, "Don't touch me. Stay away from me."

She recoiled, her face falling as she withdrew into herself. The rest of the dinner was quiet, no one daring to speak of the tension that was suffocating the room. I glanced at Mike and Elena, who exchanged worried glances, but said nothing.

The night felt like a final chapter—a moment that cemented what we both knew: we couldn't go on like this anymore. We were done, and there was no going back.

As we returned to the hotel after the tense dinner, I walked to our room while Stella went with Elena and Mike. I could hear their voices muffled through the walls, but I stayed in my room, sitting on the edge of the bed, running my hands through my hair. My mind raced with the same questions I had been asking myself for months, "What am I doing wrong? Why does she get so angry over the smallest things?"

It felt like we were stuck in a loop, and no matter how hard I tried to make things better, we kept spiralling deeper into this mess.

Mike must have sensed the tension because I overheard him speaking softly to her. "Stella, you know Noah cares about you more than anything. He loves you, and you won't find anyone who would treat you better than he does."

But she remained quiet, her silence heavy with unresolved emotion. I couldn't tell if she was absorbing what he said or just dismissing it entirely.

Hours passed, and I waited, not sure if I wanted her to come back or if I'd rather be alone. When she finally knocked softly and came in, I could tell she wanted to talk. There was a vulnerability in her eyes, a hint of the old Stella, the one I fell for.

"Can we talk?" she asked, her voice almost pleading, but I was too worn out, too frustrated.

"No," I said, pulling the blanket over me, turning away from her. I heard her sigh, the disappointment clear, but I didn't have the energy to deal with it anymore. I shut my eyes, hoping sleep would take me away from this suffocating situation.

In Her Eyes

Moments later, though, I heard her on the phone. My heart sank as I recognized the name. Paul. She called him—again.

I tried to ignore it, but the more she spoke to him, the more the jealousy, anger, and insecurity gnawed at me. Her soft laughter, the way her voice softened when she spoke to him—it felt like a punch to the gut. She talked to him for what felt like hours, each minute feeling like an eternity as I lay there, pretending to sleep, my mind racing.

'What am I doing here?' I thought to myself. 'Why am I still trying to make this work when she's clearly still attached to someone else?'

I wanted to get up, to leave the room, leave the hotel, leave her. But something kept me rooted in place. Maybe it was hope, maybe it was fear of the unknown, or maybe it was just the remnants of the love I still had for her. Whatever it was, I stayed, enduring the sound of her voice as she talked to Paul deep into the night.

I felt trapped in a cycle I didn't know how to escape. The worst part was that I wasn't sure if I wanted to.

The morning after that restless night, I woke up with the weight of everything we had been through pressing down on my chest. As I dressed, I could feel the tension hanging in the air like a storm about to break. When I saw Stella, she looked distant, her face unreadable.

"What did you want to talk about last night?" I asked, trying to break the ice, hoping for some sort of closure, some explanation for all that had happened between us.

She glanced at me briefly before looking away, her voice flat and devoid of emotion. "Nothing. Just leave me at the airport."

Her words stung, but I nodded silently. There was nothing left to say, apparently. I drove her to the airport, the silence between us heavy and suffocating. As soon as I dropped her off, she walked away without looking back, and just like that, she was gone.

I thought that was the end of it, but as I returned to Zermatt, my phone buzzed. She had blocked me on WhatsApp, but she still called.

"Did you reach home?" she asked, her voice calm, as if nothing had happened.

"Yes," I replied curtly. "But I don't want to talk right now."

There was a pause on the line before she sighed, her frustration evident. "Everything is spoiled now," she said, her tone resigned, but still sharp with lingering anger.

I took a breath, holding back the flood of emotions that threatened to spill out. "Look into yourself, Stella. Improve the things that caused this. It didn't have to end like this."

Her voice hardened, cutting through the phone like a blade. "I'm like this only, Noah. I won't change."

I couldn't take it anymore. The constant cycle, the pain, the never-ending arguments—it was all too much. Without another word, I hung up the call and blocked her, feeling a strange mixture of relief and sorrow wash over me.

In Her Eyes

As the sound of the rain against my window filled the silence, I realized that maybe this was the end we both needed, even if it wasn't the one I had wanted.

When Elena called me that day, I wasn't expecting to unravel like I did. "How have you been, Noah?" she asked gently, her concern evident in her voice.

I sighed deeply, unable to hold back the flood of emotions any longer. "I'm shattered, Elena. I don't understand what went wrong. I tried, I really tried. But nothing seems to make sense anymore."

"You've always been kind to her," she reassured me, her voice calm but firm. "But, Noah, you need to keep yourself together. She doesn't deserve you, not with the way she's been treating you."

"I don't know, Elena," I said, my voice cracking. "Maybe it's me... maybe I drove her away."

Elena paused before speaking again, a hint of something more serious in her tone. "No, Noah. It's not just that. Stella's blind by the dream of going to the USA. She's talking to Mohit because he fits into that plan. She wants to leave everything behind for some fantasy life in America."

I felt the ground slip from beneath me. "What?" I asked, my voice barely a whisper. "She's talking to Mohit because she wants to go to the USA? That's why?"

"Yes," Elena replied softly. "She's set on it, Noah. She thinks her future lies there, even if it means leaving everything behind—including you."

A cold sense of despair washed over me, my heart sinking deeper. "I can't leave my parents, Elena. I won't. I like my life here. What's wrong with it?"

"Nothing," Elena said firmly. "Nothing is wrong with your life. You've built something solid here, and anyone who can't see that isn't worth losing yourself over."

I nodded, though she couldn't see me. The weight of everything pressed down on me, the realization sinking in that Stella's dream and mine no longer aligned. And no matter how much I loved her, I couldn't chase after someone who was determined to leave everything I cherished behind.

That conversation with Elena weighed heavily on me. I couldn't stop thinking about what she said—about Stella's dreams of leaving everything behind, of chasing a life in the USA, a life without me. It felt like the final blow, the confirmation that we were on paths that could never meet again.

I spent days in a fog, going through my routine in Zermatt but feeling detached from everything around me. The mountains, the crisp air, the familiar streets—it was all there, but I felt like a stranger in my own life.

I kept asking myself why I was still holding on. Why, after everything—after all the hurt and the fights, after she'd pushed me away again and again—was I still clinging to this idea of her? Maybe I thought I could fix things, or maybe I was just afraid to let go of what we once had. But the truth was painfully clear: the Stella I loved was no longer the person standing before me.

As much as it hurt, I knew I couldn't keep chasing after her. I had a life here. A life I loved. My parents were here, my home was here. And I realized, finally, that I couldn't sacrifice that for someone who wasn't willing to stay.

In Her Eyes

9. Remnants

When Elena called me after more than a year, I had long buried the memories of Stella, or so I thought. I hadn't contacted her since that last call. It had been more than a year of silence—long enough for the wounds to scab over, but not long enough for the scars to fade.

Elena's voice on the phone sounded concerned, and I could hear the weight of what she was about to say. "Noah," she began, "I think you should know… Stella isn't doing well. She and Paul were getting along, but out of nowhere, he blocked her. The next day, he posted about getting married. She's completely devastated."

Her words hit me hard, though not in the way I would have expected. Part of me felt relieved, like some cruel cosmic justice had been served. But another part—the part that had once loved her so deeply—felt a pang of sadness, too. Even after everything, hearing that she was broken like this made me feel something for her.

I decided to visit her in Grindelwald, where she'd been living and working remotely from her parents' home. It wasn't an easy decision, but something pulled me there, a sense of unfinished business maybe. When I arrived, her parents recognized me immediately. They welcomed me with the kind of warmth I hadn't expected after all the time that had passed.

"We're glad you came," her mother said, her eyes heavy with worry. "She hasn't been herself."

Her father added, "She's taking therapy, but… it's slow. There's hardly any improvement."

I felt a knot tighten in my stomach as they led me to her room. The last time I'd seen Stella, she was full of fire and passion, even if it was sometimes misdirected. Now, as I stepped into her room, the sight of her was almost unrecognizable. She sat quietly on her bed, her face pale, her eyes distant. The vibrant energy that once defined her seemed drained.

I sat beside her, unsure of what to say. The words felt too small for the weight of the moment. "Stella," I began softly, "what's done is done. You have to let it go. Paul… he wasn't meant for you. You'll find your way again."

She didn't reply, not a word. Her silence was deafening. I could feel the chasm that had grown between us, the one created by time, distance, and all the things we never said to each other.

Her parents looked at me with hope in their eyes, but I didn't know if I had the power to help her. I wanted to tell them that I didn't have the answers, that maybe no one did. But I stayed, offering what little comfort I could in the presence of someone who used to mean the world to me.

In Her Eyes

For a few days, I stayed with her in Grindelwald, helping her through the rough patch. I took her to her therapist, made sure she ate, and stayed by her side when she needed someone to lean on. Some nights, I would sit by her bedside, watching over her as she slept. We grew close again, but there was something different this time. It wasn't the same closeness we had before. Now, it felt more fragile—like we were both trying to hold on to something that had already slipped through our fingers.

After a few days, I flew back to Zermatt. Every day, I called her, asking if she had eaten, if she'd gone to therapy, if she was feeling okay. She always answered, but there was something distant in her responses. Then, one day, she asked me, "Noah, would you come to the USA with me? I want to settle there, leave everything behind, and just be with you."

Her words hit me like a wave. "No," I replied, not even needing to think about it. "I can't leave my parents here alone. Life is good here, Stella. What is it in the USA that you can't find here?"

She sighed, and I could hear the exhaustion in her voice. "I just want to get away from all of this," she said. "Everything that happened. I just want to start fresh, the two of us."

For the next six months, I stayed committed. I called her every day, made sure she was okay, and helped her through her depression. But slowly, something began to change. I started to notice that she was online for long stretches, and when I'd try to call her, the line would be busy. At first, I thought nothing of it, but as the days passed, I started to feel like I was being pushed aside. I'd call, and it would be hours before she'd respond. The panic attacks that I thought I'd overcome began creeping back into my life.

One day, I couldn't hold it in any longer. "Stella," I asked her over the phone, my voice trembling slightly, "who are you talking to so much? You're always busy."

There was a pause. Then she answered, "It's John. He's an investment banker in New York. We're thinking of getting married."

Her words felt like a knife to my chest. "Married?" I barely managed to choke out.

"Yes," she said, her voice steady. "I always dreamt of living my life in New York. I want to leave all this behind—Paul, everything. I need a new start, Noah."

My heart pounded in my chest, and suddenly I couldn't breathe. Panic gripped me so hard that I had to sit down. She kept talking, but I couldn't hear her anymore. Everything felt like it was crashing down around me. After all the months of helping her, of staying by her side, she was moving on—again. This time, not just to someone else, but to a whole new life.

We fought. I was angry, hurt, betrayed. "You always come close when you need something," I told her bitterly. "And then, when you're feeling better, you push me away. What am I to you?"

She didn't respond, and in that silence, I realized the truth.

We stopped talking after that. Months went by. And then, one day, as I was scrolling through Instagram, I saw her post. It was a picture of her and John, smiling, happy. The caption read: #Engaged.

In Her Eyes

The final blow. She had moved on—completely, this time. And I was left to pick up the pieces once again.

Four months had passed since I last heard from her, and then, out of nowhere, my phone rang late at night. I saw her name flash on the screen, and for a moment, I hesitated. But I answered.

"How are you, Noah?" her voice sounded fragile, like a shadow of the girl I used to know.

I took a deep breath, unsure of where this conversation was headed. "Where are you?" I asked.

There was a long silence on the other end. Then, softly, she said, "Nowhere. I'm lost, Noah."

Her words hit me like a punch. "Lost? What do you mean? Are you in New York?" I asked, feeling the familiar pang of concern.

She didn't respond right away, but then I heard her weeping softly. It broke me in a way I didn't expect. "What happened, Stella? Talk to me."

Between her tears, she finally spoke. "John and I... we're not together anymore. He wasn't a good person. He left me alone, Noah. He's in New York, living his life, and I was just... just left behind." Her voice cracked, and I could feel her pain bleeding through the phone.

I clenched my fists, my anger rising. "What do you mean? What happened?"

"He had an affair," she confessed, her voice barely above a whisper. "He was only after my father's money. My family found out, and we ended things. We had already done the court marriage, but it's over now. I'm... I'm divorced, Noah." The word hung in the air like a death sentence.

Hearing that, I felt sympathy, pity, and an overwhelming sense of déjà vu. Despite everything that had happened between us, despite the pain she caused me, I still cared. I couldn't help but want to protect her, to be there for her like I had been before.

Without thinking, the words slipped out of my mouth. "Would you marry me, Stella?"

There was a pause, and I could hear her catch her breath. "Noah," she replied softly. "I can't stay here. I want to get away from everything. Would you leave your parents and come with me?"

Her question hung in the air like a heavy weight. I knew my answer, the same answer it had always been. "You know I can't," I said, my voice firm but filled with sadness. "I can't leave my parents. They're everything to me. Life is good here, Stella. You don't have to run."

But it was clear that she had made up her mind. "I understand," she said quietly.

I felt my heart breaking all over again, the rollercoaster of emotions crashing down on me. I needed to protect myself, to finally move on. "My parents are looking for a girl for me," I said, trying to regain control of my feelings. "If they find someone good, I'll say yes. I've waited enough, Stella."

There was a long silence on the other end. Then, with a soft voice, she simply said, "Okay."

In Her Eyes

And with that, she hung up the phone. I stared at the screen, feeling a mix of relief and heartbreak wash over me. This time, it felt final.

10. Last words

A few months after things ended with Stella, I got engaged to Tessa, the girl my parents chose for me. Our families got along well, and Tessa, though not Stella, was someone I could respect and trust. She was loyal, kind, and carried herself with a quiet grace that made it easy to like her. She wasn't my past, but she felt like a future I could grow into. We posted the news on Instagram—engaged—and I tried to put everything behind me.

But it didn't stay buried for long. Despite blocking each other, Stella somehow found out through a mutual friend. One evening, out of the blue, she texted me.

"I want to marry you. I want to have kids with you. I want to build a house and settle down with you. I want to grow old with you, Noah, and die in your arms at 110. I want a lifetime with you."

Her words pierced through me. I stared at my phone, my heart racing. After all these years, she was saying everything I had once wanted to hear. But now it was too late.

I replied, "I wish this could happen, Stella."

Moments later, my phone rang. It was her. I hesitated but answered.

"Will you marry me, Noah?" she asked urgently, almost pleading.

"Stella…" I began, unsure of what to say, but she interrupted me.

"Will you?" she repeated, her voice trembling with impatience. "I want to spend my life with you, Noah."

Tears welled up in my eyes. I couldn't contain the emotions that surged through me. "It's too late, Stella," I said, my voice breaking.

"Will you marry me, Noah?" she insisted again, this time her voice cracking under the weight of everything unsaid.

"What is this, Stella?" I asked, not knowing how to process what she was doing. My mind was racing, my heart aching with a mix of regret and longing.

She let out a shaky breath. "If I don't say this now, I'll regret it for the rest of my life. Will you be my husband?"

I choked back my tears. "I wish I could say yes."

"No more wishes, Noah. Just answer me. Yes or no. I won't say a word after that. Just answer."

I closed my eyes, the weight of everything pressing down on me. "Stella, the decision has already been made. Our families… everything has already been set."

Her voice softened but stayed steady. "Okay, I understand. I just want you to be happy, Noah. With or without me, you deserve happiness."

I felt my heart splintering. "Stella, I've waited to hear this from you for so long, but now that it's finally come, it hurts."

"I know," she said quietly. "I wanted to say it when my heart felt right. It's always been there, Noah, this feeling. I just couldn't accept it. I love you. I've loved you forever, and I still want to be with you. It doesn't matter where we live."

I could hear the desperation in her voice, the rawness of her emotions. "I wish time was right," she added softly. "Give us a chance if you can."

I shook my head, knowing it couldn't be. "You know it can't happen, Stella."

"I don't know that, Noah," she said, her voice rising with a last flicker of hope. "I don't think it can't happen. You think it can't. I'll be waiting for you." Her words lingered in the air, heavy with finality. "Goodbye. Take care. And if your answer is no, don't call me back. I'll make my heart understand."

"Shut up, Stella," I whispered, tears falling silently.

"You shut up, Noah," she shot back, her voice catching in her throat. "Take care. It'll take time, but it'll be fine. I'm serious, Noah—never call me again. If this is really it, just... don't."

I wiped my eyes, my throat tight with the weight of goodbye. "You'll always be in my prayers, as you have been."

In Her Eyes

"Please don't reach out to me," she pleaded, her voice softer now. "It's not right. You're engaged. Give her all your love and respect."

"Why are you doing this?" I asked, though I already knew the answer.

"I'm not doing anything," she said quietly. "I can't do anything anymore, Noah. I can only wait and pray for your well-being."

With that, she hung up. The silence that followed felt like the end of an era—a finality that I hadn't been ready for, even after everything. I stood there, phone still in hand, my heart heavy with everything we could've been, but never would be.

A few minutes later, my phone buzzed. It was a text from Stella.

"Can you send me her pictures?" she asked.

I scrolled through my gallery, finding photos of the engagement. I sent them to her, and then waited for her response.

A few seconds later, her reply came: "She's beautiful. Okay, bye now. Don't contact me. My phone will be off. Don't worry about me."

Tension built up in my chest. I couldn't stop myself—I called her immediately, twice. Both calls went unanswered. My heart raced, panic rising, and then her text came in again.

"Don't have a heavy heart, don't bother about me, Noah. It's okay to have thoughts, it's okay to have emotions. I want you to have peace. I don't have such a big heart that I can talk to you after you're with someone else."

Naman Porwal

I read those words over and over, feeling a lump in my throat, each sentence hitting harder than the last.

"If you're not with me, you should be with her wholeheartedly. I'll say it again—I love you, and I'll wait for you, but I'll accept whatever you do. You're mature enough. Let me know if I can do anything for you. I'll be more than happy."

My heart felt like it was breaking all over again. Even in this moment, she was trying to be strong, to give me her blessing—something I had yearned for but now felt utterly heartbreaking.

"Take care, don't cry over me. You need to be strong. All the endeavours are waiting for you. This will be my last message to you, Noah. I can't take it anymore. Bye. Love you."

Her final words crushed me. I sat there staring at my phone, feeling a void open up inside me, as if the final chapter had truly closed on everything between us. I wanted to call her, tell her how much she had meant to me, but I knew this was her way of saying goodbye for good. She couldn't take it anymore, and in truth, neither could I.

I wiped away the tears that had fallen unnoticed, trying to process the weight of it all. For the first time, I realized this was the end of a chapter I had held onto for so long. Now, it was time to let go, even if it shattered me in the process.

That night, as the rain poured relentlessly outside, I found myself alone in my room, staring blankly at the window. The sound of the rain echoed my emotions, a storm of memories and heartache swirling inside me. As I sat on the bed, lost in thought, I noticed an envelope tucked away in the drawer. It was a letter from Stella, sent on my birthday months ago. I hadn't opened it. Maybe I wasn't ready then. Maybe I'm not ready now. But something made me reach for it.

My hands trembled as I unfolded the paper. The rain outside seemed to grow louder, as if the night itself was preparing me for the weight of her words. I began to read:

Happy Birthday,

You. Yes, you—the most important person, my truest friend, my deepest soul, and the best gift life ever gave me. You brought me back to myself, taught me how to love who I am again, and made me realize how lucky I am to have you. You've always taken care of the little things I never even thought mattered, but they mattered to you because they were about me. You made me smile again when I thought I had forgotten how. You made me a better person.

First, thank you. Thank you for walking into my life when you did. I know we fight, sometimes too much. I know we go silent and irritate each other to no end. But that's because with you, I feel safe enough to be my most honest self, in ways I can't be with anyone else. You're the one person who loves me for who I am, without needing me to change. Do you know how rare that is?

Noah, you're not easy. You're not everyone's cup of tea. But I don't need anyone else to endure you, because that's my privilege. You're different, you're precious in ways that are hard to explain. I pray every day that you soar, that you achieve something incredible, whether I'm beside you or not. I wish more than anything we could celebrate every birthday together.

Love you, my stubborn dog. Yes, you drive me mad. You irritate me, and yes, we fight—but don't ever think that weakens us. It only

Naman Porwal

makes us stronger. I love you more than the moon, more than the stars, more than I can ever express. I don't ever want to let you go, because I'm not sure I'd survive it. You mean the world to me in ways I can't even begin to put into words.

Thank you for being you. For loving me the way you do. For letting me be exactly who I am. Happiest Birthday, Noah—the boy who loves neon colours, who loves me fiercely, and who was never meant for this ordinary world. I love you, always. And now, I even love your neon too.

Forever, Stella

As I read her words, the weight of it all hit me harder than I expected. Every line felt like it was pulling me back, unearthing the love I tried to bury, exposing the raw emotions I had hidden. The rain outside seemed to echo her words, steady and relentless, like the love that had never truly left. Tears welled up in my eyes as I clutched the letter, her voice echoing in my mind. It was too late now.

I sat there, staring out into the rainy night, wishing for a time that was already gone. The rain kept falling, as if it would never stop.

ABOUT THE AUTHOR

Naman Porwal is not just a Chartered Accountant from Indore but also an accomplished author whose journey began with a tapestry of personal experiences. Drawing inspiration from real life events, he translated his thoughts into quotes, which laid the foundation for his debut book, *Feelings of Mind Connected to Heart*, a remarkable achievement considering he was only Seventeen years old at the time. With over 10,000 copies sold, the book resonated with readers and marked the inception of Naman's book writing.

Following this success, Naman continued his literary exploration with his second book, *I Still Love You*, published in 2020 and his third book, *Where Love Happens*, published in 2024. The books received significant acclaim, showcasing Naman's ability to capture the nuances of love and relationships.

Naman's philosophy revolves around the synergy of hard work and smart work, a belief he embodies in both his professional and creative pursuits. His work garnered attention to the extent that Notion Press offered him the opportunity to present his book at the New Delhi World Book Fair 2019, where it received enthusiastic praise from young readers. The book became one of Notion Press's bestsellers.

Naman has not only achieved success as an author but has also been honoured at various award functions for his remarkable feat of publishing his first book at the young age of seventeen. His popularity extends beyond the literary realm, as he is known for his guitar skills and a passion for reading and writing. Readers and enthusiasts can connect with Naman Porwal on Instagram (@wherelovehappens) or via email (nicenaman123@gmail.com). His engaging narrative style and insightful perspectives continue to captivate audiences, making him a notable figure in the literary landscape.

ACKNOWLEDGEMENTS

I would like to express my deepest gratitude to my parents, for their unwavering love, encouragement, and support throughout my journey in writing this novel. Your belief in me has been a constant source of inspiration, and I am endlessly grateful for your guidance and sacrifices. Thank you for always being there for me, cheering me on, and believing in my dreams.

To those who doubted me, criticized me, or wished for my failure, I extend my sincerest gratitude. Your skepticism and negativity fueled my determination, driving me to prove you wrong and strive for excellence. It's time for you to clap, for your doubts only served to strengthen my resolve and propel me forward.

Thank you to all those who have supported me, believed in me, and cheered me on along the way. Your unwavering faith in my abilities has been instrumental in bringing this novel to fruition. This journey would not have been possible without each and every one of you.

Naman Porwal